LEAVING HOME

Flora Canning's bags are packed. She's ready to begin a fresh life in New York, leaving her handsome friend Richard Cross devastated at her departure. But plans don't always work out, and a family tragedy forces Flora to stay a while longer. Then fabulously wealthy Nate Campbell enters her life with an offer most women couldn't refuse, and Flora has to learn who to trust and whether it is better to rule with your head or with your heart.

*Books by Cara Cooper
in the Linford Romance Library:*

SAFE HARBOUR
TAKE A CHANCE ON LOVE
THE SANCTUARY
HEALING LOVE

CARA COOPER

LEAVING HOME.

Complete and Unabridged

LINFORD
Leicester

First published in Great Britain in 2009

First Linford Edition
published 2010

British Library CIP Data

Cooper, Cara.
   Leaving home. - -(Linford romance library)
   1. Single women- -New York (State)- -
New York- -Fiction. 2. Love stories.
   3. Large type books.
   I. Title II. Series
   823.9'2–dc22

   ISBN 978–1–44480–222–1

Published by
F. A. Thorpe (Publishing)
Anstey, Leicestershire

Set by Words & Graphics Ltd.
Anstey, Leicestershire
Printed and bound in Great Britain by
T. J. International Ltd., Padstow, Cornwall

This book is printed on acid-free paper

1

Flora zoomed the zip shut around the bulging suitcase and stood up to gaze around her house, empty now apart from basic items of furniture.

'So, you're really going to do it?' Richard asked.

'Yes,' asserted Flora. 'This time I am and *nothing* is going to stop me.' She was wearing vibrant purple, a no-compromise colour.

'I'll miss you.' His blurted words froze Flora's smile and she couldn't meet his eyes. People so often said 'I'll miss you,' without really meaning it. But she could see Richard, dear friend, constant companion with the kindest eyes was struggling to keep his emotions in check.

'I'll miss you too.' She met his gaze, then dropped hers immediately when she saw the hope which sparked in his eyes. It would be cruel to lead him astray. She knew Richard hoped for more, had always hoped for more and she just couldn't give it. Richard was her confidante, her untiring supporter. He could have been her soul mate, they had a lot in common. But Flora had done with soul mates. She firmly believed you could only have one of those in your life. And Damian had been hers. Just for a short while.

Momentarily she allowed herself to remember Damian, a fleeting snapshot of him flashed across her memory like a long forgotten photo falling out of a book. She pushed the image out of her mind and focussed again on Richard. No. What Richard had to give wasn't what she needed. Particularly not now. Not now her bags were packed, and her mind made up after so many years of wanting a different life. At last all her plans were in place and ready to come to fruition. And it felt fantastic.

As Flora rifled through her documents and passport neatly folded in her handbag, checking one last time every-thing was there, she marvelled at how she'd managed to be so focussed once her decision was made. Her little Victorian terrace house had been emptied of trinkets, all sold on eBay or given to the charity shops. It felt so good, like having a massive spring clean, to discard things she'd been hanging on to for years. She'd de-personalised the house with a fresh coat of bright white paint. Tenants, the lettings agent had told her, paid more for something neutral and classy. Flora was exhausted with months of decorat-ing, making everything perfect for the newcomers. After all, the tenants who would be arriving next week were going to pay the rent which would finance her new life in New York.

Flora had made everything spick and span, sewing new sofa covers and matching curtains. She was so grateful for the sewing skills she had learnt at design college all those years ago. They had never come in so useful. The basic furniture looked sparkly new. Totally impractical for most people, it had nevertheless suited the smart professional couple who had decided to rent Flora's house at a premium.

Flora looked at her hands, red from smartening up her beloved garden. She had clipped and weeded everything, and spent her last pennies paying a builder to cover the lawn in low maintenance decking. She'd even saved enough to have the tiny front area where she parked her bicycle tiled in black and white squares and the crumbling wall replaced with railings to make it inviting — 'kerb appeal' they called it — with two clipped bay trees in terracotta pots to complete the look. The house had never looked better but strangely, it didn't feel like hers any more. Perhaps that was because her head was already somewhere else, way across the seas in America.

It was time for Richard to go, her flight was leaving early next morning, but it was clear he didn't want to. He scuffed the back of his heel and stood on one leg like a stork before settling back into his usual relaxed stance, hands in the pocket of his denim jacket.

'So, you're sure this job you've got out there in New York is actually going to come off? I wouldn't want to think of you stuck in a strange city without any money. It's all so sudden.'

Flora laughed, not unkindly. 'It's not sudden at all Richard, you know I've been working for months getting everything ready, and for years planning this. Yes, the job's secure. I got a letter from the Panton Trust on Monday giving me a start time. I really am going to be Artist In Residence at the Hughes-Renton Museum of contemporary art in Brooklyn.'

'It's a world away from teaching art in a South London comprehensive.'

'I've had enough of teaching teenagers, I've wanted to be a proper artist since I came out of college. Teaching was only meant to last a couple of years and it ended up lasting ten. I'm twenty-nine years old Richard. If I

5

don't do it now I never will.'

'You're leaving all us plodders standing Flora. The Hughes-Renton Museum sounds very grand.'

'It's not grand. In fact it's a tiny museum and I'll only get paid a stipend. I shall have to waitress in Greenwich Village in the evenings. I'll be exhausted but for once I'll feel fulfiled. The Hughes-Renton is doing the most wonderful innovative work and amazingly, they loved my paintings.'

'I love your paintings.' Richard's normally jovial face was dead serious. 'I miss not seeing them on the walls. It's a sin you locked them away in storage. Your house doesn't look the same. It's not cosy any more.'

Now was the time, thought Flora. The time to say a final goodbye and give Richard his present. She pushed behind the curtain covering the hallway window and took out a large flat package wrapped in brown paper tied with string. 'This is for you.'

Richard gulped as he took it, and silently, reverently untied the string letting the brown paper slip to the floor. As the canvas was revealed, bright oranges and purples, greens and electric blues leapt out of the painting, startling in the plain white hall. Richard gasped. 'It's gorgeous — your garden in spring. Oh, and there we are, sitting under the lilac tree, just you and me.' There was a long pause. ' . . . Flora, I . . . I got something for you too.'

'You didn't need to.'

He took a small box out of his pocket, wrapped in purple, her colour. He knew her so well. For one moment, Flora felt the blood drain out of her face, and for a second she felt terrified. The box was just the right size for a diamond ring. She swallowed hard and peeled off the paper. Relief flooded her veins, and a tinge of something which felt almost like regret. Inside the box, sitting on a velvet cushion was a golden charm in the shape of an artist's palette with a delicate paintbrush fashioned in gold laid across the palette. Blobs of colour across the palette were tiny gems: a blue sapphire, a red ruby, a yellow topaz glistened up at her. The end of the brush had been tinted with purple enamel just as if it were oil paint waiting for an artist to start a canvas. It was exquisite.

'Richard this is too much.'

'No,' he shook his head. 'All I ask is that you wear it often and remember, I'm always here when you need me, however far away. I'm always here.' He had been there for her so many times from his house across the road from hers. There when she needed to borrow tools for the garden, there when she had problems with her internet connection, there when she wanted to try out a new recipe.

As she watched him go across the road giving her one last wave and close his front door, her next door neighbour Jenny Deeds opened her door to put out the recycling. Jenny was chubby with dark hair and her little toddler,

Olivia, known to all as Lolly eagerly bustled around her feet. As Jenny lifted the lid off the bin and put in used envelopes, Lolly proudly took them out. Flora tried a bright smile, to cover up the sadness of watching Richard go. 'I see you've got your little helper there.'

'Helper, more like a hindrance, but she does like to do her bit, don't you darling?' Lolly's tiny bunches wiggled as she nodded her head then began carefully to tear each envelope in half, then quarters, then scatter the bits like falling leaves over the pathway.

Leaning down to help pick them up, Flora said, 'How you cope Jenny? What with Lolly and the twins. I heard them crying earlier, I guess you managed to get them down in the end.'

Jenny's husband worked nights and all the overtime he could get in order to keep his growing family.

'Oh yes, they go down eventually. They're no trouble, and I did so want a boy. When nature sent me two, it was like a bonus.' As she spoke, Jenny

9

absent-mindedly removed quantities of torn up envelope, which Lolly had decided to taste, from the toddler's mouth and wiped it with a tissue. 'No, Lolly, don't. Dirty.' Jenny made an icky face and the little girl imitated her, making both Flora and Jenny laugh.

Flora watched Lolly career off down the short path, to stand like a little prisoner with her tiny fists closed over the gate leading to the pavement. She peered out with fascination at the street lamps and the breeze whirling the bare branches of the trees. At that age, thought Flora, everything was tinged with wonder. With her minuscule bunches dancing in the wind and her cosy pink romper suit, Lolly looked like a living doll. Lolly jumped up and down, pointing and exclaiming, 'Puss, puss,' the gate clanking as she shook it and watched a cat on the other side of the street.

Across the road, Richard drew the curtains and suddenly everything seemed so terribly final. Jenny followed Flora's glance. 'He'll miss you.'

'He'll be fine,' replied Flora.

'I'm not so sure,' mused Jenny. 'There are some men who need a person to look after and he's one of them. That guy needs a wife and a ton of kids running around. It's a shame to see a good man go to waste.'

'He'll find someone.'

Jenny looked at Flora and sighed. 'Like I say, he'll miss you. We all will, are you still intent on going?'

'That's my bags all packed and ready now. I'll write, and send photos.'

'It's not the same is it? You're leaving us all behind and going off to the bright lights and big city. I'd love to go to New York.'

'You love it here, Jenny. You've got everything you need with your growing brood. There's plenty of time to go to New York on holiday some day. You can come and stay with me.'

'Hah, chance'd be a fine thing with all these little ones; they'd drive you crazy.' As Jenny spoke, Lolly decided for some reason it would be a good idea to twirl round and round endlessly like a tiny dancer in a music box, which she did until she fell over her feet and thudded to the ground, cushioned only by an over-sized nappy. Looking startled, she picked herself up and wobbled dizzily over to her mother crying, 'Feel sick Mummy,'

'Oh, oh,' Jenny scooped Lolly expertly up into her arms. 'Time we went. Flora. If I don't see you before you go tomorrow good luck.' The two women embraced swiftly, each seeing the tears threaten in each other's eyes, then Jenny whisked Lolly back into the house.

Flora hesitated long enough to see the light go on in Richard's bedroom, then closed the door behind her. She wondered, not for the first time, whether she was making the right decision in leaving these familiar things behind. She mustn't falter now.

She locked her front door preparing for the last night she would spend in her house. She would sleep well. Like a caterpillar waiting to turn into a butterfly. Tomorrow her exciting new life would begin. A bubble of panic launched in her chest but she inhaled deeply, chasing it away. Her mind was 110 per cent made up and the feeling was so exhilarating, it made the hairs on the back of her neck tingle.

Flora set her alarm for 8am. Snow was on the weather forecast for tomorrow and lots of it. Luckily, her flight was at lunchtime, before the snow was forecast to start. Her taxi was booked for 10am. By the time the snow came her plane would be up in the air zooming off to a new life. She settled down to sleep in a bedroom which didn't seem like hers any more, and watched the moon emerge for the last time over the end of her garden. The next time she would see the moon, she would be in Brooklyn.

2

Sleepily, Flora was aware of something invading her dream. She squeezed her eyes closed. The noise wasn't her alarm, it wasn't morning yet, it was still black outside. She turned over, but the noise didn't stop. She leaned her arm out and felt a vibration as her hand alighted on her mobile phone. Forcing her eyes open, she stared at the flashing phone. Ten minutes past two in the morning. Who on earth was phoning at this time?

Fumbling on the touch screen and putting the phone to her ear, she heard a disembodied male voice taut with urgency. 'Hello, hello?' he said over and over like a stuck record.

'Hello,' she managed, her voice was thick with sleep. 'Who is this?'

'Is this Flora Canning?'

'Yes. Who is this, do you know what time it is?'

'Yes, Miss Canning, I'm aware of the time and very sorry to waken you.' The voice was businesslike and sounded as if it was owned by someone who had all the troubles of the world weighing on his shoulders.

Flora sat up in bed and leant forward. Her head rushed and she felt dizzy. 'Well, why did you then?' she asked somewhat rudely.

'I'm sorry, Miss Canning. I have some very bad news.'

Flora was finding it hard to get her head together. Her thoughts were jumbled like the pieces of a jigsaw, not making sense. 'What's wrong? Is my flight cancelled? Oh no, please don't say that.'

There was silence at the other end and Flora forced herself to sit up on the side of the bed. As she put her bare feet on the floor, a jolt went through her at its coldness. Her turquoise pyjamas felt thin in the chilly air and she held the collar up under her chin.

She was suddenly aware that the

15

normally rumbling sound of traffic from the nearby road was muffled. Flora pulled on her slippers and shot over to the window to see wafts of white flakes battering horizontally at the window pane like insects trying to get in. She shivered as an icy blizzard forced its way through the gaps around the glass.

Parked cars in the road were loaded with what looked like white icing on cupcakes. Snow — snow everywhere.

As she focussed, she saw a black cat picking up its paws and shaking them irritably as it stepped gingerly under the orange street lamp. The snow was easily up to its tummy. Four or five inches must have fallen. And it was still falling thickly.

Flora realised the voice on the other end of the phone had gone silent. 'Are you still there?' she asked.

'Yes, Miss Canning. I'm not calling about your flight. I'm calling from East Holdington General Hospital. I'm afraid there's been an accident.'

'An accident?' Flora's brain was in gear now. But she didn't know any East Holdington. It wasn't near here. She held her forehead trying to make sense of all this, while the wind flipped in the other direction, swirling snowflakes around the streetlamp like crazed confetti.

'Two people are . . . ' there was a hesitation, 'two people have been involved in a pile up, on the motorway. I believe they are relatives of yours. A man and a woman.'

Flora shook her head. She had so few relatives.

There was an aunt and an uncle up north but they were quite aged now and neither of them were drivers. Flora's father had died when she was young and her mother had married again. Flora's stepfather had taken his parental role very seriously and been strict with Flora but he had tried to be a good father substitute. Sadly her mother had been a heavy smoker and had succumbed to cancer when Flora was in her early twenties and her stepfather had died a few years later.

'Who? I'm sorry to be dense, I don't know where East Holdington is. Are you sure you've got the right person?'

Flora could see a front door open across the road, and watched the cat rush in to the comfort of a warm house.

'The young lady . . . ' Flora could hear the man swallow hard, 'the young lady who passed away gave us all your details before . . . well, before she died. She had a letter from you in her handbag, it has your phone number on, that's how we contacted you.'

Flora felt as if she'd stepped into a surreal canvas where nothing was the right shape and nothing added up. She frowned. The man's voice intoned very slowly as if he was speaking to someone foreign. 'Megan and Ryan Souter. Do you . . . did you know a Megan and Ryan Souter?'

As if she had received a blow in the chest, Flora stumbled backwards, landing heavily on the bed. She held her hand to her mouth. 'Megan. I haven't seen Megan in eight years. She's my stepsister. We hardly ever speak, just send Christmas cards. I had a Christmas card from her only a month ago. I don't understand, it can't be her.'

'I'm so sorry, Miss Canning. She was brought in with a fatal injury. She didn't suffer. Our paramedics were able to administer painkilling drugs as soon as they got to the scene. But . . . but they weren't able to save her or her husband. He died on impact. But she was able to tell us in the hour she was in hospital while we tried to save her, that you were her next of kin.'

'Yes . . . I suppose I am. Oh poor Megan. And Ryan, he was such a lovely guy. I can't believe it, it's too much to take in.'

'Please accept my profoundest sympathies Miss Canning. There's no easy way to get such news. But there is a small ray of light.'

How could there be? Flora's mouth was dry. As she unclasped her fingers and saw the red indents of her nails in her palm she realised how she'd held her hand in a tight fist all the while the man's unreal words had floated down the phone.

As she stared at the wild snowflakes still dusting the window pane, Flora could see an image of how Megan had looked the last time she'd seen her. At Flora's own twenty-first birthday. Megan had worn a lime green chiffon dress and had looked like a wood sprite with her slender legs and long dark hair. Without a shred of makeup, Megan was a strictly soap, water and no frills girl. But she didn't need any frills; she'd been as natural as a flowing stream and as wild as a dark wood.

No one told Megan what to do or how to do it. When she'd met the love of her life in her teens, she'd upped and married him only weeks after they'd met, unworried about what the world thought. Ecology and nature were her two passions and Ryan and Megan had retreated to a cottage in Wales.

The last letter Flora had had from her had literally oozed bliss. They had fixed up the leaking roof, restored the fireplace and put in a wood-burning stove. They were growing vegetables and soft fruit. Ryan was making just enough to keep them both from his job as a carpenter. And Megan was in seventh heaven pottering about their little cottage.

Megan was busy in her domestic bliss, and Flora was busy doing her teaching. Gradually their letters to each other had become less regular and dwindled until they just sent each other Christmas cards. In the early ones, they each said that they must pay a visit. But Wales was a long way from London, and it never quite happened.

Flora had always thought the next thing she would receive would be an invite to a christening, but it never happened, and she hadn't wanted to pry. Some people couldn't have children and others didn't want them.

Flora herself had never wanted to be

a mother. She was convinced she would be rubbish at it, and didn't even keep a pet.

When she got immersed in her painting, whole days and nights could go by where all she did was paint and then nap. The creative urge, when it grabbed her, didn't let go until she'd finished a canvas.

If Flora had had children, she knew there would be a conflict between her creativity and her child and that was a battle she didn't want to fight.

Flora wondered if that was why she held her friend Richard at arm's length. He came from a family of five and had endless nephews and nieces. Richard's life plan had always involved children at some stage, although he'd never really gelled with any of his girlfriends and lately had been reluctant to find another.

A sudden blast of wind against the window dragged Flora back into the present. 'What do you mean? What possible ray of light could there be?'

The man's voice was kinder, less official now as he said, 'Miraculously, their baby girl survived, without a scratch.'

'What baby?'

'The baby was with them. Harvest. Strange name but I guess as she was born in October it seemed appropriate. It does sort of grow on you and she has that lovely corn-coloured hair. Is that why they called her Harvest?'

'I don't have any idea what you're talking about.' Flora gathered the bedclothes over her knees as if this was a dream and she wanted to wake up, without any snowstorm raging outside and without any deranged man on the phone bringing unwelcome news. 'Who are you anyway?'

'Oh, I'm sorry Miss Canning. I should have said, I'm the surgeon who treated your stepsister. My name's Mr Greig. Please accept my apologies. We've had an awful time up here with accidents in this dreadful weather. I'm hardly making sense am I? But I'm short of staff, many of them haven't made it through the snow and I wanted you to know about the accident and your stepsister and brother-in-law's death immediately. Particularly with the baby only being four months old. Your stepsister gave me your details before she died and told me how she had left provision in her will for you to look after the baby in the event of anything happening to her and your brother-in-law.'

'Me? But I didn't even know there was a baby. I'm stunned.'

'I'm sorry if this has all come as a shock to you. I take it you and your stepsister weren't particularly close.'

'No. I mean there wasn't a rift or anything. We are — were — far apart in age, she was years younger than me. Megan was just very busy with her life and I was with mine. I wonder why she didn't write and tell me about her having a baby.'

'She told me she felt guilty not contacting you for so long. That you were keener on writing letters and she was the one who tailed off first. She was worried she'd been a bit selfish, wrapped up in her own things. She asked me to apologise to you.

'There wasn't much time when she came into hospital and she knew it, she could feel herself getting weaker. But she did say that the only reason she hadn't told you about the baby was simply that she'd been so busy and she wanted to surprise you with some professional photographs she'd had taken. She was sad that she hadn't yet seen them herself. But the baby, Harvest, needs you, Miss Canning. She needs a mother.

'There are a few formalities to go over with the police and social workers but that will have to wait. Everyone's so short staffed with this bad weather. But the baby's here, whenever you're ready to come and collect her.'

Words rattled around in Flora's head. She wanted to protest, declare that there was no way on earth she ever wanted to be a mother. That hadn't been part of the plan. Other women were mothers. Women who didn't have a desire to follow their passions. Women with husbands. Flora just wasn't one of those women and that little baby was not her child. It was a stranger. And what's more Flora had a world of plans a million miles away that a baby could never be part of.

The wind dropped and the snow was now drifting down like white rose petals almost as if they were in mourning for Megan. Flora sat watching the snow as if this was happening to someone else. She felt something drip from her cheek onto the duvet cover. A single tear. She didn't sob, she was too numb for that. Everything was falling apart around her.

When she finally forced some words out of her mouth, they were flat and in a monotone. 'This is a lot for me to take in now, Mr Greig. Please, I know you're terribly busy, but I don't seem to be functioning very well.'

'Of course, that's understandable.'

'Would you mind giving me your phone number at the hospital and I'll get back to you tomorrow. That will give me time to think.'

Mr Greig agreed, once more adding his condolences and rang off. As Flora sank back into the bedclothes, the silence added to the unreality. The world had shifted on its axis and was spinning out of control and there was absolutely nothing Flora could do about it.

3

When Flora awoke to the alarm the next morning a feeling of euphoria rushed through her at the thought of flying to New York. Then, instantly, seeing the snow piled up on the window ledge, her spirit plummeted as she remembered the phone call in the night, and that everything had changed. That her dream had been usurped by an impossible reality. She had difficult decisions to make. To go or not to go to New York. To accept she was now going to look after the baby or to decline and let the authorities deal with Harvest.

Flora's limbs felt heavy as she dragged them out of bed and a nausea settled in her stomach. There in the bathroom, the shelves were empty and her toilet bag was neatly packed as if mocking her.

What on earth was she to do? She felt

as trapped by her situation as a hamster in a cage. After washing, she dressed in the clothes she had carefully laid out for the flight — a pair of grey cashmere leggings, a chunky white aran knit jumper and suede ankle boots — and made her way downstairs. She'd bought a croissant and had left a spoonful of fresh coffee in the cafetiere yesterday, all ready for a quick, trouble-free breakfast.

In a daze, she carried on with the routine she had planned for herself. She ate without tasting, telling herself that she needed to be quick to catch her flight. It was like being two different people, the real her who was single and independent and had a new future waiting for her in New York. And the unreal her, a woman who has been told that a relative she had barely thought of in years had just left her with another life to care for.

Flora pushed away the half eaten croissant and looked at her house, all bright and fresh like a new pin and she could feel the ache in her back from all that decorating.

She had worked hard for her dream, darn hard. So why should she change it? She felt awful for her stepsister, Megan, but frankly, Megan had been wrong in naming her as the best person to look after the baby.

'I'd never make a good mother,' Flora said to herself. 'Not in a million years.' Surely she didn't have to take Harvest on.

What a strange name that was for a child. Romantic and airy-fairy and head-in-the-clouds just like her stepsister. It was typical of Megan to make decisions without consulting anyone. If she had consulted Flora, she would have been firm in telling Megan the truth — that she was not a born parent and that there were thousands of other people who would do the job much better than she ever could.

That was it then. Flora would phone the surgeon and tell him she wasn't able to take on Megan's little girl. That the law would have to take its course and decide on some other way to care for the child. Guilt washed over Flora, but she pushed it aside. No, this situation wasn't her responsibility.

Suddenly, as she took her plate and mug to the sink, Flora felt as if she were walking on air. All the burden, all the liability had slipped off her shoulders and after drying the dishes she stretched fully.

Yes, she had made her decision and she was going to stick by it. You only had one life. She had decided the life she was going to lead and it didn't consist of giving up her art, ditching the job of a lifetime and looking after someone else's baby. Your stepsister's baby, said a little nagging voice at her elbow.

'Anyone's baby,' she said out loud to the empty air.

She picked up her mobile to phone the surgeon but somehow it wasn't quite that easy. She put it down again.

She had bags of time and it was still

very early. He'd been up half the night, he probably wasn't back on the new shift yet. She would wait a little longer. She wandered over to the window.

Everything was done. She had time to kill before the taxi came. Then she remembered Richard's charm still in it's box. She was wearing a plain chain around her neck. Undoing it, she slipped the charm onto the fine chain and put it back around her neck. Feeling it there was a comfort to her somehow.

Flora looked at the snow. It had come down all night and there were still flurries even now. She frowned and went to the back door and opened it.

It was like opening the door to a massive deep freeze. On the top of the fence post was a settling of snow that looked just like a top hat and was just as tall. Flora had never seen so much snow fall in London. She listened intently. Even though this was the middle of the rush hour she could barely hear any cars.

Closing the door, Flora hurriedly switched on the TV and listened to the newsreader who was standing on a bridge overlooking the M25, clouds of snow battering her jacket. 'And here, in Surrey, the M25 is moving very slowly. There is a severe weather warning. All the major London airports have been closed after a plane came to an emergency stop on the runway which was obliterated by overnight snow. Passengers are stranded, and more snowfall is expected. The severe weather is coming straight over to us from Russia. The only places which will escape the worst weather today are the South West and Wales.'

Flora felt her heart beat quicken. They must be wrong. Some flights must be going out today. Flora flicked through her papers for the airline's phone number and punched the digits into her mobile. Sure enough, there was a recorded message saying that all flights had been suspended.

Despair flooded through her. Her

resolve to leave, to fly away and start her new life, to be somewhere else as soon as possible was being snatched away. She could drive herself to the airport and simply wait for the first flight out. That was it, that was what she would do.

She grabbed her grey woollen coat off the hook, wound on her scarf, and flung her handbag over her shoulder. Seizing her suitcase, Flora opened the door and plunged into six inches of snow. She hadn't stopped to put on sensible boots and her suede ankle boots let in the snow immediately. But Flora was determined — wet feet were the least of her problems.

The car was unrecognisable under its ridiculous snow hat. Hastily, she pushed away the snow which was hiding the handle and opened the door. A little avalanche crashed off the roof and onto the driver's seat. She brushed it off hastily, feeling her gloves cake in crunchy ice. Working in a frenzy she managed to clear first the front then the back windscreen. The snow on the roof would have to stay, she didn't have time for that. Slinging her case in the back she got in and turned the key.

Silence. She turned it again. A cough this time, a splutter, then silence. Again she tried. This time a wheeze, then silence. Flora turned the key again, and again and again. So intent was she that she didn't see the figure in jeans, heavy tan boots and a navy blue polo neck come to stand next to the driver's door. The door was opened and there was Richard, snowflakes sticking to his streaky blonde hair then melting into droplets.

'You'll flood the engine if you keep that up. I'm afraid it's had it. What on earth are you up to anyway? Can't you see no one's going to be going anywhere today?'

'I have to,' Flora stated, 'I'm taking myself to the airport. I can't believe things are that bad.'

'It's bad, Flora.' Uncharacteristic lines of concern etched themselves between Richard's eyes. 'I even checked on your flight just to see what was happening. There's no way it's going today, nor tomorrow, the flights'll be totally backed up. I know you were all set to go but they'll understand in New York if you're delayed.'

'I have to go, you can't stop me.' Flora wrenched the key around in the ignition once again, like a woman possessed.

'Flora, what's up? This isn't like you to be unreasonable. Something else has happened, I can tell.'

Drat Richard, thought Flora. He could read her like a book. He was right. Her urge to escape an impossible situation was making her unreasonable. She placed her hands on the steering wheel, rested her head in its centre and let out a wrenching sigh.

She felt a light, almost imperceptible touch on her hair. Richard's hand, held for a second, long enough to show his concern, was lifted away again as he said, 'Flora, tell me what's happened.

Even if I got the car started now, it'd be madness to set off in the snow on your own. Come and have a coffee and tell me what's up. I'll share my last packet of hot cross buns.'

When Flora looked up, Richard's smile was so warm, she had to give in. He lifted her case out of her car and carried it inside, his feet crunching in the snow. In moments the coffee machine was on, the hot cross buns buttered and Flora's unsuitable footwear was drying on the radiator.

It felt good to be in his house; masculine, but still cosy. She'd always liked his décor — the Eucalyptus wood floor he had laid himself, and the leather sofas. Her voice breaking, her feet tucked up in an armchair, she told him of the telephone call she had received in the night.

Richard's handsome face, still tanned from his recent skiing trip, looked at her mixed with concern and disbelief. 'That's awful for you. Your poor stepsister. I know you weren't close but it must have been a dreadful blow. And a baby! Wow, that's some legacy! Poor kid.'

'I don't know what to do Richard. What I really wanted was to run away. To get a flight, any flight so that I could turn my back on everything. And now I'm stuck. Am I being terribly selfish?'

'No,' he considered. 'It wasn't wise of your stepsister, not to tell you about the baby. And crazy of her not to ask you about taking on her child. Maybe that's why she took so much time getting around to telling you about Harvest. Perhaps she was afraid you'd turn down being named as her guardian and she wanted to re-establish contact with you and broach the subject gradually. Then, events just took over.

'There must have been something about you that persuaded her you'd be the best mother substitute her little girl could have.'

'I very much doubt that.' Flora hadn't thought of it that way. Megan

38

had always been flighty and unpredict-able. Flora doubted that much thought had gone into Megan's decision. 'I wish she'd asked me and given me the chance to turn the offer down. I'd be rubbish. I can't do it. I don't want to and no one can make me.'

'True. They can't. But why not look on this delay as a positive thing.'

'How?' Flora threw her hands up.

'Sometimes things are just meant to be. Maybe, being delayed by the weather gives you thinking time you wouldn't otherwise have had. Where's the hospi-tal where the baby's being looked after?'

'In Wales.'

'Maybe we should take a trip there.'

'What? Five minutes ago you were stopping me travelling. And I've just told you I've made up my mind, Richard. I can't look after Harvest.'

'Now wait, just wait.' Richard put his hand up. He was a gentle man but persuasive when he wanted to be. 'What I actually said was that it would be madness to travel alone, particularly in your little car. I've got the 4×4 and it's just been serviced. A bit of snow won't trouble it at all. The weather forecast says the snow is going to ease off in the West, so if we set off soon we'd actually be going away from the bad weather not into it.'

'We? What about your work?'

'The boss phoned me to say he's told the whole office to stay at home. We'd find it hard getting up the hill into the office in this weather and I don't think he wants people getting stuck there overnight.

'It's a sensible decision, but I suspect he's keen to get out with his kids and enjoy the weather. The schools are all off. But us poor lonely singletons don't have anyone to play snowballs with so all I'd do is sit here and eat hot cross buns. So really,' he continued with a twinkle in his eye, 'you'd be saving me from myself.'

Flora looked at his figure, lean from cycling, well-toned muscles from eve-nings spent at the gym and she knew

Richard wouldn't waste his day overeating. She wasn't keen on trekking to Wales but in some ways it might be a blessing. Trust Richard to look on the bright side.

At least then, when she turned down the suggestion of taking on the care of little Harvest, it wouldn't seem that she was totally selfish.

She could discuss with the surgeon and the authorities what would happen to Harvest. Then, after a day or so the flights would be going out to New York and she could continue as planned.

'How long would it take?' she asked anxiously, not sure of the distance.

'Four, five hours maybe. We'd be there by lunch time.'

'Are you absolutely sure Richard? It's an awfully long way.'

'It'll be an adventure. I know they say you shouldn't travel unless you have to but this is an exceptional circumstance. Besides, I've just finished a huge piece of work at the office, been burning the midnight oil carrying out a large audit

41

on a shipping company. I could do with a break from my desk.'

Richard was an auditor for a local accounting firm. Flora knew he worked like a slave so perhaps she might be doing him a favour giving him an excuse to get away for however short a time.

'Okay. I suppose doing something's better than hanging around here all packed with nowhere to go. It's the least I can do for Harvest. I'll bet when I get there I can't even hold her properly. I'm nervous around babies. I don't have a single maternal bone in my body.'

Richard laughed as he cleared away their things and got his heavy sheepskin jacket on. As a precaution, he put a shovel in the back of the car and a flask full of tea. The 4×4 was made for rough terrain, it would definitely be up to the journey.

Once they got going, the snow started again. It hit the windscreen, with the wipers going full force for an hour. Then, as they started heading properly West, the skies began to lighten a bit and the snow turned to sleet and didn't settle so much on the grass verges along the motorway.

As she watched the fields and towns shoot by, knowing that Richard's calm, capable driving was getting them safely on their way, Flora felt her eyelids grow heavy. An interrupted night, the humming of the 4×4 and the heater pumping out were all she needed to send her off to sleep.

4

Richard only took his eyes off the road for a second to peer at the sky. It was touch and go, he could see that. He fixed his gaze back on the lorry in front. The weather forecaster had said that Wales wasn't going to bear the brunt of the snowstorms but Richard had a suspicion it wasn't going to be long. The sky had that yellowy look that heralded heavy snow. This cold front was set to cover the whole country.

His conscience pricked him. Should he have been so ready to offer to take Flora away from home? He honestly believed that if the cold front moved slowly, they could still get to Wales, see the baby and return within the day. Without the baby, if that was the decision Flora made, and in time to catch a flight to New York once they opened the airports again — tomorrow or the next day.

But could Flora return without Harvest? Could she really leave the baby to an unknown future? He simply didn't know. Sometimes he thought he knew Flora and sometimes he realised he hardly knew her at all. There were aspects to her personality that Flora kept hidden, so protected behind a brick wall of resistance that he wondered what she feared.

He couldn't help thinking that in going to New York what Flora was really doing was running away. From what he didn't know.

They had reached a busy exit on the motorway, and the traffic had ground to a standstill. He took the opportunity to look at the girl sleeping by his side. He'd always thought she was beautiful.

From the first day he saw her chatting and taking out coffee to the removal men as they loaded her stuff into the house across the road. She looked arty and interesting. She was one of those women who was effortlessly elegant and who simply didn't know it. She'd worn her hair pinned off her face that day, in a carelessly constructed upstyle that framed her elfin features.

Even in her moving gear of black leggings and an oversized t-shirt he could tell she had fabulous legs. She was small and neat and as she laughed at the removal men's jokes, her voice carried across the road and through his open window. It was summer then, and the scent of honeysuckle had mingled with the sound of her chatting.

He decided he would knock on her door that evening, once she'd settled in and welcome her to the street.

But she'd beaten him to it. He was making coffee after his evening meal and trying to buck up the courage to knock on her door when his front door bell rang. She'd stood, hair trailing down her back, damp from a recent shower. Devoid of make-up, her eyes were large and sky blue. 'Sorry to disturb you, but I've just moved in over the road.'

'Oh right?' He'd feigned disinterest, embarrassed by the fact that he'd spent most of the last hour thinking about calling on her.

'Do you have a telephone directory. Something's up with one of the taps and I need a plumber. I'd usually check for one online but my computer's not set up yet.'

'You're welcome to come in and use mine. Would you like coffee?'

They had taken their coffees onto the patio and sat chatting until the sun went down. Their conversation flowed and she laughed easily. He had watched as her damp hair had dried in the summer warmth, and fell into soft waves as it did so. She'd told him how she had taken a teaching job in a school which was known to be facing problems and had challenging pupils, and how terrified she was at standing up in front of a class of teenagers.

'I always think they'll catch me out, ask me something I don't know and then laugh or even walk out saying they'd rather play football than mess around with paints and paper and clay. It's difficult to get kids' attention nowadays. They've always got their mobiles out texting their friends or they're plugged into their iPods and listening to music.'

'I would have thought art would have been one of the subjects that appealed to them most. I'm sure you'll do well.'

She'd thanked him that night and said he must come over for a bottle of wine sometime. White was her favourite and they'd since enjoyed many a bottle of chilled Pinot Grigio while they'd put the world to rights.

But somehow he'd never got to asking her out though he'd often wanted to. She'd put up the barriers early on, saying how she wasn't looking for a boyfriend after having her fingers badly burnt with a relationship she didn't care to talk about.

He had contented himself with being a friend, a trusted, loyal, good friend. At least he could be around her, enjoy her company. Flora had seemed pleased for him on the few occasions he'd announced he was going on a date. But none of the girls he'd met had occupied his thoughts half as much as Flora did.

He looked over at her now as she breathed steadily, in a deep nap. The fringe on her forehead made her look like a schoolgirl even though she was nearly thirty. Her long pale blonde hair tumbled round her shoulders in those waves like primrose petals shimmering in an Easter breeze.

He smiled thinking how often she'd threatened to cut it short but he'd talked her out of it. She looked peaceful now whereas she'd looked troubled in the past few months as she'd battled with the decision to give up her job and take the one in the States.

A sudden squawking in the sky ahead forced Richard out of his reverie. A gaggle of seagulls whirling noisily across the sky made him frown. They were nowhere near the coast, those birds must have come inland because the weather was taking a turn for the worse.

Richard gazed back at Flora, hoping they'd get to their destination safely. As he looked at her, he noticed a glint of gold at her neck. There was the gold charm he had given her of the painter's palette with the little coloured gems. Exhilaration surged through him.

She'd taken the bother, troubled as she was this morning, to find a chain on which to hang the charm. And she'd planned to wear it on her flight to the States. Maybe he did mean something to her. Maybe she did see him as more than a friend.

Her small, pale hand sat in her lap. He desperately wanted to lean over, fold it in his and see whether it was warm. He couldn't bear the thought of her being cold. He stretched out his hand, hovered it over hers then brought it back. He mustn't take advantage while she was sleeping. If he was ever going to be lucky enough to hold her hand, he'd want to be looking in her eyes at the time.

He sighed, leaned over to the back seat, grasped the car blanket and gently laid it over Flora's knees and up to her neck.

The traffic began to clear and started moving again. Richard fixed his eyes on the road resolving not to take them off it until they reached their destination. What's more, he told himself, stop wasting time thinking about things which will never be.

★　★　★

By the time Flora woke, the snow had reached Wales in earnest. Fat flakes coated the roadside, and three inches had fallen in an hour. They were winding their way through Welsh market towns, with people grabbing their coats around them against the chill.

They passed a school where a caretaker was putting up a notice saying 'Closed Until Further Notice'. The children ran out, catching snowflakes in their mouths. It was heartwarming to see their delight at having an unexpected 'snow day'.

Parents were turning up with sleighs as shops started to close early too. A snowball, higher than the children themselves, was already being pushed along by them. A group of mothers stood and chatted merrily, some of them in brightly striped scarves, protecting a pile of discarded satchels, all school work forgotten as the children played.

Flora and Richard had made reasonable time and decided to stop for a late lunch. Flora had been only too keen to agree that they eat before going to the hospital. She had found her empty stomach plagued with butterflies at the thought of meeting the surgeon.

After roast Welsh lamb with all the trimmings, Flora said to Richard, 'If you don't mind I think we ought to get going now.'

His chocolate brown eyes were full of compassion. 'Are you sure you're ready for this Flora? It seemed like a good idea this morning but I'd quite understand if you weren't up for it.'

'No, Richard, I'm fine. To back off now would be silly. I have to face this problem, for Megan's sake and for Harvest's. I don't know what my decision will be. I'm still set on New York. My heart's already there. I've got a list of locations I want to see and paint. Central Park, the Flat Iron building, Liberty Island, the Staten Island Ferry.

'In my mind I'm already in my tiny apartment in Brooklyn, already working at the museum. I've even started paintings in my imagination — I've done all the preparation, chosen the colours and the themes — I just have to bring them to life. I can see all the vibrant colours of New York jumping out at me. Wales isn't for me, it's dark here, the light's flat, it's no place for a painter.

'And babies aren't for me either. But it's only fair to Megan's memory to come here and see the baby, if only to check that she's okay and say goodbye before I go away. If I know she's in good hands and someone's taking care of her I'm sure she'll be better off with them than me.'

Richard didn't answer. He reached for her coat, helped her into it and said, 'Come on then, let's go.'

★ ★ ★

It was a small cottage hospital on the outskirts of town. Confused as to which was the entrance, Flora and Richard went in through the A&E door. 'My, it's busy for a small place,' Richard muttered as they searched around for someone to ask for the right ward.

But everyone was rushing around and the waiting area was fit to bursting. Children sat crying on their fathers' knees and old people were assisted by nurses who were rushed off their feet.

As they looked around for a notice-board with a map of the wards on it,

Flora spotted a desk headed *Information* with an elderly lady sitting underneath the sign. 'Let's go and ask.' There were three people in front of them. Finally it was Flora's turn. 'You're very busy today.'

'We certainly are, it's been mayhem ever since the snow started. Little ones have been coming in after smashing their sledges into tree trunks and loads of people who misjudged the iciness of the pavements have slipped. I pity the poor doctors and nurses. I just heard the buses have been stopped from going out, and the railway lines have been iced up over an hour so the new shift of medical staff can't get in. People are wonderful, they're offering to do overtime and sleep in if necessary, but a lot of them are dog tired.'

'Goodness,' said Flora, 'we've been lucky in having an all weather car, and the main roads are still functioning. At least you made it in okay.'

'I'm just a volunteer, and I'm lucky to live over the road and came here as soon as I got a call. I haven't seen this much snow in years.'

Flora and Richard got in the lift and went up to the second floor. It wasn't quite so frantic but the absence of staff was still apparent as the reception desk on the ward was deserted.

'We'd better walk around and see if we can find Mr Greig.' Discreetly, without waking any of the patients, Flora and Richard went around the ward until they found an office with a glass window set into the door. Inside sat a weary looking man with grey hair, who was just finishing a telephone conversation. He put the phone down, and looked up questioningly, beckoning them in.

'Can I help you?' His manner was brisk, he obviously had a lot to do.

'I'm Flora Canning, we're looking for Mr Greig.'

As she mentioned her name, Mr Greig's face changed and a relieved smile spread across it as he reached out his hand gripping Flora's warmly. 'Miss

Canning, delighted to see you, delighted. And Mr . . . ?'

'Richard Cross, I'm a neighbour of Flora's and her chauffeur for today.'

'Good of you to drive in such awful weather. I can't tell you how pleased I am you made it. As you can see, the hospital's gone crazy. Poor little Harvest really isn't getting the attention she needs but she's a good baby, a real sweetie. Oh, Miss Canning, I'm forgetting myself, I should have offered you my condolences on your stepsister and brother in law . . . I . . . it's always difficult at times like this to say the right thing, but I want to stress that your stepsister didn't suffer. The paramedics got to her quickly. Unfortunately your brother in law was killed on impact but although your stepsister was with us a while longer, she responded well to the painkillers and was very comfortable in her last moments. I am most sorry for your loss.'

Flora swallowed, she hadn't been looking forward to this encounter for a number of reasons. If the surgeon were too kind to her she would start to cry. She felt the tears prick the back of her eyes. The baby, she must focus on the baby, that would take her mind off Megan.

'Thank you Mr Greig, you're kind. I'm so grateful that you were able to talk to Megan, that must have put her at ease.'

'What put her at ease, my dear, was knowing that she had named you as Harvest's guardian. There was only one other person she talked about in respect of Harvest's care. A Mr Nate Campbell, he's well known around here, a youngish chap — very wealthy I'm told, through buying and selling property. He was at school with your stepsister's husband, Ryan and has a holiday cottage next door to them. Apparently he and Ryan were very close and Mr Campbell had offered to help pay for Harvest to have private schooling but that is something you will have to take up with Mr Campbell personally.

'Your stepsister spoke very highly of you, she told me how sensible you were and that you work with children. She thought that was a good sign and that being a teacher would stand you in stead to understand little ones.'

Whoa, thought Flora, they were moving way too fast. Mr Greig obviously thought she had made a final decision and that she was going to agree to take Harvest away for good and bring her up.

It was so complicated. All of a sudden she had been catapulted into Megan, Ryan and Harvest's lives and here was Mr Greig talking to her about this Nate Campbell who wanted to help.

A short while ago, Flora hadn't even known she'd had a niece and now everyone was asking her to organise the baby's future. All Flora had wanted to do was to see Harvest, make sure she was okay and check that someone would be found to take her on.

'Actually, Mr Greig, I teach teenagers.

I have no experience with babies. They're a complete mystery to me and I'm not sure I'm equipped in any way to look after Harvest. I was due today to fly out to take up a job abroad. I'm really not sure that I can acquiesce to my stepsister's wishes. She didn't check with me before she named me her guardian and frankly if she had I would have declined. And as far as sending her to private school, well, any sort of school is a long way off.'

Mr Greig looked crestfallen and moved back behind his desk. 'You'd better take a seat Miss Canning.'

Flora and Richard sat down. Flora felt distinctly uneasy, and guilty at the fact that she hadn't agreed instantly to take Harvest on.

Mr Greig looked Flora in the eyes and steepled his hands in front of him. 'Miss Canning, I have to tell you as a surgeon at a busy hospital, it is a daily occurrence for me to see people like yourself who are facing extraordinary circumstances. Birth, death, illness are my stock in trade. I admit I had hoped that you had come up here to claim Harvest and take her to a loving home. I jumped to conclusions and that's a bad thing. One thing I would say is that I hope you will not make any hasty decisions.

'Being in the midst of tragedy and upset is not a good place from which to make life changing decisions. Especially those which radically affect others. I can see your situation is extraordinary. You are single and you have your own life to lead. You were at a crossroads in your life before all this happened. You've had a shock and you're worried about being landed with responsibilities that had never been on your horizon.

'But I'd urge you to weigh things up carefully and to think very hard about your future and about Harvest's. There are many women for whom a baby is a wonderful gift. Any new life is a miracle. New life is precious. I urge you to search within yourself to try and take the right decision for everyone.'

Suddenly, Flora felt a great weight sitting upon her. Of course Mr Greig was right. She couldn't rush this decision. But still, she wanted to run away. She gulped. 'What will happen to Harvest if I can't be her guardian?'

He pursed his lips. 'I'm no social worker. I couldn't say for certain. But I guess she'd be put in care. Maybe a children's home or foster carers. Or I suppose she could be put up for adoption. Babies are very sought after. But I couldn't say for certain. Her future would be the subject of case conferences and huge amounts of red tape before a decision was made. She'd go into the system and have to work her way through it.'

The room fell silent. The only sound which drifted up from below was the rumbling engines of the ambulances pulling into the entrance of A&E. Flora didn't know what to say. She hadn't thought past the moment when she had planned to see Harvest, confirm to herself that she never wanted to look after a baby, and shook Mr Greig's hand to say goodbye.

Social workers, adoption, bureaucracy, red tape. She hadn't thought of any of those. They sounded hideously impersonal and she wanted nothing to do with them. A lump welled up in Flora's throat. The enormity of her situation threatened to overwhelm her until she heard Richard speak.

'Thank you for those wise words Mr Greig. It might help if we could see the baby and perhaps Flora and I could talk things over. As you say, it's not a time to make rash decisions.'

'Of course,' Mr Greig nodded. 'I understand all this is very difficult. Take as long as you need. If I had any ancillary staff to spare I would see if we could get you a coffee, but there's a machine at the end of the passageway where you'll have to help yourself. I'll take you to meet Harvest and you can take her in the waiting room, get yourselves a drink and talk it over eh?'

They got up and followed Mr Greig

down a short passageway and into a brightly painted room. A window looked out over a green with a tree in the centre, bare of leaves and heavy with snow. In the corner, lying in a cot lay a bundle covered with a white blanket. Mr Greig silently left them. Flora went a few paces before she stopped, turned, and looked at Richard. 'She's so quiet,' Flora whispered. 'Surely we shouldn't wake her if she's sleeping.'

'Don't worry. Just go over and take a look,' he urged.

As if needing to delay things, Flora laid down her handbag, took off her coat and placed it on one of the armchairs. She was hot, and aware that her hands were sweating. In that cot lay a bundle of responsibility, a real live tiny person needing serious looking after.

Flora wished she could grab her coat and be gone. The baby was doing fine here. She had everything she needed. Flora just felt her presence would be an interruption. As she stood rooted to the spot, she suddenly felt a cautious hand in the small of her back, urging her on. Like someone walking exhausted up a steep hill she needed Richard's hand gently pushing her forward to the next step.

As Flora approached the cot, she noticed movements then saw impossibly small pink bootees wriggling out from underneath the blanket. But the blanket was over Harvest's face. Immediately, Flora felt a panic rise within her. Surely poor Harvest would suffocate with the blanket over her like that. Where were the medical staff to look after her? Instinctively, she reached out her hand and pulled the cover back.

Flora was met by a smile so radiant it filled the room. Harvest had perfect apple-red cheeks and skin like strawberries and cream. Her corn-coloured hair which was sticking to her forehead stood out on the pillow like a sunburst. 'Oh gosh,' Flora gasped, 'she looks just like Ryan.'

Richard came around to the side of the cot. 'Apparently nature makes it that way, for them to look like their fathers I mean. It's so that the father will bond with and protect the child.' He reached his hand inside the cot. The baby's eyes followed him as he offered her his forefinger. Five tiny fingers with nails like little seashells grasped Richard's finger and held it fast.

'She's a strong little thing,' he said. 'And hot. Here, feel under her chin.'

Tentatively, Flora reached in and placed her hand on Harvest's neck. 'Oh heaven's, she's overheating. What shall we do? Maybe we should call a nurse, she's got a terrible fever.'

'No she hasn't Flora, she's just a bit hot that's all. Babies are like that. I remember looking after my baby sister while Mum cooked the dinner. Mum always had a hand knitted cardigan ready so that it could be popped easily on and off. Babies find it difficult to regulate their own temperature, particularly when they've been sleeping. It's fine, just take the blanket off, pick her up and pop her on your knee. She'll soon cool down.'

'Pick her up? Oh I couldn't. I don't know how.'

Richard laughed. 'It's easy. Just lift her under her armpits, lift her up and quickly support her bottom with your hand. She'll be fine.'

Flora reached into the cot as if she were being asked to pick up a priceless antique. She shifted around to get the right position before doing as Richard had explained and grasping Harvest under the arms. The baby stared at Flora as if to ask who this stranger was.

At least she hadn't started crying. Gingerly, Flora took Harvest's weight. Holding her at arm's length, the baby sailed in mid air, all chubby legs and wriggly feet. Flora couldn't work out how to turn Harvest's body round to get ready to sit down and put her on her lap.

Richard leant against the wall, arms crossed, keeping his distance, and trying to suppress the smile that threatened to turn into a laugh. 'You're enjoying this, aren't you Richard Cross? I really don't know what to do with her. She's going to start crying any minute, I know it.'

'No she isn't. She's as good as gold. Look how patiently she's waiting even though you've got her hanging there like a rag doll.'

'Oh Richard, look, her head's lolling backwards, I've broken something.'

'You haven't broken anything, she's leaning back to look at the lights in the ceiling. Babies love light or anything that sparkles or moves. She's discovering the world, that's all.'

'She's slipping, I'm losing her.'

'No you're not, stay calm. Sit down and land her on your knee. There, that's right. See, she's fine, she likes you.'

Sure enough, once Harvest had landed safely on Flora's knee, she rewarded her with a bright smile and a gurgle of happiness.

'Phew, I'm boiling hot, is it hot in

here or is it me?'

'Actually, it's you. You really aren't good with babies are you?'

'I kept on telling you.'

'You'll get better. It's all a question of learning. I'm off to get us a cup of coffee. See you in a few minutes.'

'Don't leave me with her.' Panic made Flora's voice squeak.

'Don't be daft, Flora,' called Richard, his voice disappearing off down the passage. 'I won't be long and you'll be absolutely fine . . . really . . .'

So there was Flora, left on her own with a tiny dependant creature about as familiar to her as an alien. Luckily, Harvest's gaze had been caught by the branches of the tree outside waving in the wind.

As she followed the moving branches with her wide eyes, she leaned out her chubby arms, clad in their white towelling romper suit. Neat little fingers opened causing dimples on the back of her hand and closed again with glee as she watched the moving branches. For the first time ever, Flora thought what amazing creatures babies were.

To most of us a tree is just a tree, something we take for granted. But for Harvest, everything was a source of wonder. Even the most mundane things had magic for her. Despite herself, Flora found herself marvelling at Harvest. She was so perfect. As she gurgled and laughed at the swirling, twisting branches, Flora found herself laughing too, watching Harvest's bright sparkling eyes, alert and lively.

Looking around, Flora felt suddenly very alone. She had stiffened with the effort of keeping Harvest in one place. So, gradually, she eased back into her chair and brought Harvest into her lap. The tiny body was warm and cuddly. Tentatively, Flora released her hold from underneath Harvest's arm and brought it around her shoulders. Instantly, Flora felt cosy and peaceful. Harvest nestled into Flora's chest, laying her head close to her body, making her wonder how long it had been since Harvest been cuddled.

'I see the two of you have made friends already. That's just what she needs.' Flora looked up to see Mr Greig standing in the doorway.

'I don't think I'm making a very good job of it, but she seems happy.'

'She's a lovely baby. And unfortunately, at this moment with all our resources stretched to the limit, you're the only one who can give her the comfort she needs.'

'Me? Oh, I'm not sure about that Mr Greig. I have to tell you, I only came here today to check that Harvest was okay. I think I'd made my decision even before I saw her that I can't keep her forever. I really don't know what I'm doing and I feel as nervous as a mouse in a cattery, I don't know what the rules are for looking after babies. Cuddling Harvest is one thing, but I don't know a thing about feeding or bathing her. I'd be hopeless.'

'The problem is, Miss Canning, that I'm so short staffed at the moment,

Harvest would have to take second place to all the other work we have. She's a good baby, she wouldn't complain, but that doesn't mean to say she wouldn't feel the loss of not having someone care for her one to one. Look, can I just make a suggestion?'

'I can't stop you doing that.'

'How would it be if you took Harvest home for a few days? You're her closest relative. Keep her for a little while, until this bad weather passes and the hospital gets back to normal. While you're there you could contact Ryan's old school-friend Nate Campbell. From what your stepsister told me, Mr Campbell wanted to contribute to her upbringing. He's a wealthy man, and unmarried. He could be a useful benefactor. At least if you take Harvest home, that will give you time to make a considered decision on Harvest's and your own future.'

'But I live miles away, it took us half a day to get here and it would take more to get back to London. I don't think it's right to take a baby miles in this awful weather. What if we broke down?'

'When I said take her home, I meant take Harvest to her home, somewhere she's familiar with, not back to your home where there are no familiar smells or sights. I have your stepsister's hand-bag with her keys and the address to her cottage. It's in the hills a bit away in one of the villages, but not far from here.

'Usually, the social workers would deal with these sort of emergencies but I can't get any reply in this awful weather and I really don't have the resources to keep Harvest here. You need only keep her for a day or two. The decision is yours, Miss Canning, but I hope I can persuade you to get to know Harvest a little before you take your final decision.'

A masculine voice from the passage-way said, 'It's a wonderful idea Flora. Driving back today wouldn't be a great idea. Why don't you take up Mr Greig's suggestion?'

Richard placed a coffee on the table next to Flora and smiled at Harvest asleep in her arms. Flora looked down on the baby. As she did so, she placed her hand on Harvest's head and stroked her hair back from her forehead. Her hair was soft like silk. The baby had cooled down nicely and seemed perfectly content. Much better than she had been on her own in the cot trying to kick her blanket off and with no one to attend to her. A delicious scent of talcum powder and soap emanated from the curled up body. In a moment of weakness, Flora heard her own voice saying, 'Yes, I'll take her, just for a day or two.'

'Excellent,' piped up Mr Greig.

'But only on one condition.' Flora's voice was firm. 'You've got to help me, Richard. I can't look after her alone. You're from a big family, you'll know what to do if I get stuck.'

A smile suffused Richard's fine features. 'Of course I can. I'm sure there's a spare bedroom in the cottage or I can sleep on the sofa in the lounge. I'd be delighted to help.'

His deep brown eyes looked intently at Flora and whilst she was grateful for his help, she wondered in that split second if she wasn't falling into the deepest hole she'd ever dug.

Five minutes ago she was an independent woman with a plane ticket to a new life in her handbag. Now she'd morphed into a woman who didn't have a clue and was asking for help from a man she didn't want to mislead into thinking she wanted anything more than his friendship. After her dreadful experience with Damian she'd finished with relationships.

What on earth had she done? Flora looked down at Harvest, who snored gently without a care in the world, ignorant of the devastating shockwaves she had sent through Flora's life.

5

Mr Greig had given Flora the keys and pointed out on a map, the way to the cottage. 'It's lovely, you'll like it. The cottage is on the outskirts of a hamlet, on the edge of a pine wood. If peace and quiet is what you like, you'll get it there.'

Actually, big city bustle is what I like thought Flora in trepidation. Still, it would only be for a few days, then she could get back to her normal life.

As they walked to the car park, Richard said, 'We really need to get some provisions in. I know you're not planning on staying long but with this snow, it would be a good idea to get some shopping done now, just a few bits and pieces to take to the cottage.'

'Of course, good thinking. Just a few small things to keep us going.'

As they drove along, Richard suddenly pulled in to a parking space in the

High Street next to an old fashioned tearoom. They hadn't shut up shop for the day — in fact they looked busy to overflowing where people had gone in to shelter from the bad weather and to get warm.

'Flora, if you stay here with the baby, I'll shoot around the shops in double quick time and pick up what we need. There's no point you and Harvest having to brave the weather.'

Flora agreed and, as she waited for him to get her a coffee, she thought how considerate he was, always thinking of others before himself. It was a wonderful quality in a friend. As she watched him chat amiably with the girls at the counter, who blushed as he joked and charmed them, she thought again, what a shame it was that he hadn't settled with any of his girlfriends, and that she wasn't interested in men after the fiasco she had with Damian.

When she was young, Flora had been self-contained, very focussed on her studies, which suited her parents who ran a strict home. Flora was never one of those girls who got into boys young. She was one of the academic crowd, happy with her books, her sport and her art. She'd done well in practically everything at school so her parents had wanted her to follow her stepfather and do a science degree. But that was one thing that Flora stuck firm on. She may have been good at sciences but they didn't enthral her.

Art was her passion and her joy. Even though her painting was excellent, her stepfather constantly pressured her to seek a career other than an artist, something solid and reliable. Megan, her stepfather and mother's child, was so ditzy, they could see she would never have a solid career, and had pinned all their hopes on Flora as the clever one. So, to please her stepfather, Flora had gone into teaching. It was at the school that she had met Damian. He was an architect who had come to present plans for the school's new sports wing.

From the moment she had set eyes

on him, Flora was smitten. He was artistic too. He had dabbled in book illustration and was good at it. But there were so few jobs in that line and they paid poorly so he had mixed a love of engineering with a love of art to become an architect. Besides, architecture paid well and Damian liked to live life to the full.

Damian loved his boys' toys, always being the first to have new gadgets, mobile phones, up to the minute cars. Flora really didn't care about all that, but she did care about Damian. His flippant, devil-may-care-live-for-today attitude to life brought her an invigorating breath of fresh air.

Her stepfather was never keen on Damian but, after a whirlwind romance, they had got engaged in secret. The day Flora had to break it to her parents, she had chosen to do so alone.

'I'm not scared of your dad,' Damian had declared. 'I love you Flora, I couldn't live without you, you know that. Your dad will just have to accept that we're going to get married and we mean everything to each other.'

'I know Damian,' Flora had looked up into his dark eyes with their heavy lashes, and stroked wayward black curls off his forehead, 'but I'm going to have to break it to him gently and I think it's best if I do it on my own.'

'Okay, Flora but I'll be waiting outside in the car. In case you need me.'

At the time Flora had been flattered. She'd looked on Damian as a knight in shining armour, ready to do battle for his mistress. If only she had listened to her stepfather on that day but by then of course it was too late. She had sat her parents down and confessed, 'I have something to tell you. Something to do with Damian and myself.'

'Yes dear, what is it?' Her mother had lit up another of her ubiquitous cigarettes, something she habitually did when she was nervous.

'Damian and I are getting married. We got engaged at the weekend. We want as little fuss as possible.'

'And as little opposition,' her stepfather interrupted.

Flora blanched, she had known this wouldn't be easy. 'Damian doesn't like people interfering in his life, he — '

'He's not good for you Flora. Can't you see that young man's far too flash for his own good.'

'Peter . . .' Her mother had pawed at her stepfather's arm to get him to stop. But her stepfather was in full flow.

'Don't stop me now, Margaret, things have to be said! I wish you hadn't taken this step Flora. I don't want to spoil your fun and I don't dislike Damian. I can see his attraction, he's handsome and he likes the good things in life. But can't you see, he's not marriage material? He's not solid, not dependable. He acts more like a man about town than a husband-to-be and I can't see that changing just because you're going to get a piece of paper that says you're his wife.'

Flora felt her hackles rise. 'I don't

know what you mean, Damian loves me, he'd never be unfaithful. Man-about-town makes him sound like he's some sort of love rat! You don't know him — '

Her stepfather had sighed and started to pace the room. 'I don't mean he'd be off with other girls. From what I've seen, he really does only have eyes for you and I understand that can be very attractive. But Flora, he's not steady, he likes having fun too much to settle down.'

Flora had stormed out and straight into the arms of Damian who had been only too happy to whisk her away. 'Forget about it, Babe. Your stepfather doesn't know what he's talking about. I don't think he's ever been young. Come on, let's go out and flash the cash and have a really nice dinner somewhere posh where you can forget about him. We're engaged, we love each other and that's all that matters.'

That evening, Damian had taken her into London and booked a table at The

Dorchester. They had had a fantastic meal in the hotel dining room and Damian had acted like a prince, ordering champagne and pâté de foie gras. It had been fun, but that evening had planted the slight seed of doubt in Flora's mind. Her stepfather was strict and old fashioned but he had always put Flora and Megan's interests and their futures at the centre of his world.

To his endless credit it had never mattered to him that Flora was Margaret's first husband's child. He had treated both girls the same and cared for them in his own authoritarian way. Flora respected him. As the bill for the meal at the Dorchester arrived, Flora caught sight of the cost and it made her gasp. She couldn't say anything to Damian, he was on too much of a high. But it did occur to her that he was like a child, living for the moment, not considering the future.

As Flora bounced Harvest on her knee in the teashop, and watched Richard navigate his way to her table, around people's bags and coats slung over chairs, she knew he wasn't anything like Damian. She knew that where Damian was reckless, Richard was dependable.

A shudder went through her at the awful pain Damian had inflicted on her. How duplicitous he had been. The man she had loved had turned out to have feet of clay and a heart full of empty promises. In the end he had lied to her and nearly destroyed her. If she lived to be one hundred, she would never trust a man again.

'You look deep in thought,' Richard said.

'It's nothing.' Flora gave him a swift smile. 'I was just thinking of my parents. Maybe it's having a baby in my arms and being aware of her future that took me back a bit. Now, if you get a pen out of my handbag, there's some paper in there and you can make a shopping list. That snow's getting thicker, the sooner we get on our way the better.'

They found Corner Cottage easily. Fifteen minutes out of the village, off the main road and round a bend. It sat, as its name suggested, on the corner of the lane. Apart from one other cottage at the end of the lane there was nothing but countryside. Behind Corner Cottage lay a pine wood, deep and thick under its white snow covering.

'It's gorgeous,' exclaimed Flora as she undid the catches on the new car seat Richard had bought for Harvest, lifting her out. For a moment she stood and stared, with the baby fast asleep beside her. 'It's like a picture in a child's storybook. My version of Hansel and Gretel had a cottage just like this, rough stone walls, rose arch around the doors, leaded light windows.'

'Here, let me take Harvest, she's heavy for you in that car seat. If you go in and make us a cup of tea, I'll bring in the shopping and your case.' Richard's feet crunched off down the snowy path.

The cottage was freezing inside, but a warm drink soon revived them. Once Richard had taken his overnight bag and Flora's case upstairs, he worked on making up the fire. In an inglenook fireplace stood a Swedish wood burning stove. There were enough logs for that evening, and a pile of kindling in a basket. Once the fire was lit, he left the door open and let the heat flow around the cottage.

'There — it won't be long before we're baking hot. Those stoves are wonderful once they get going.'

Flora had found the teapot and cups and had brought in a tray and laid it on the large leather stool in the centre of the room which doubled up as a coffee table. She sat down and stared at the flames licking around the logs. 'Are you okay?' asked Richard. 'It must be very strange for you coming into your stepsister's house and seeing all her stuff around.'

'It is, but only because although it belonged to Megan it's like being in a stranger's house. I was eleven when Megan was born. She came along just as I was beginning secondary school. I had loads of friends and used to do a lot of sleepovers, and at the weekend I had my sport, so we really didn't see a lot of each other.

'Once she started school she was going off at the weekend to kiddies' parties and I was starting to be interested in teenage things like going to gigs at the local clubs and becoming independent.

'Megan and I got on really well, but we never spent a lot of time with each other. I mainly remember her on the beach holidays we had together in Wales with Mum and Dad. I guess that's why she decided to live here when she and Ryan got married, because it had such good memories for her. I'm glad she was happy, the cottage has good vibes.'

'Ah, and look who's waking up.' Richard lifted Harvest out of her car seat to have a good stretch, before handing her to Flora. Immediately,

Harvest's face crinkled up and she emitted a cry, which turned into a wail.

'What's wrong with her?' Nothing could raise Flora's blood pressure quicker than hearing those cries. 'She sounds as if she's in agony.'

'I think what you're hearing,' laughed Richard, 'is the sound of a hungry baby who's woken up with an empty tummy.'

'Here, have her back, I'll go and get her something to eat.' Flora deposited Harvest unceremoniously in Richard's lap and escaped to the kitchen. While the baby exercised her lungs, there was the sound of cupboards opening and closing frantically until Flora came back, running tense fingers through her tousled hair. 'You've got to help me Richard, what on earth do four month old babies eat?'

'They don't,' chuckled Richard.

'They must eat something.'

'Milk, that's all they have at this stage. Although she's probably ready to be weaned. I bought some powdered milk, it just has to be made up, and the bottles sterilised.'

'What do I do then, boil them or something?' The panic in Flora's voice mingled with Harvest's hungry cries.

'No, that will take forever. Here, you take Harvest and I'll show you.'

Flora carried the noisy wriggling Harvest into the kitchen and watched Richard deftly take sterilising equipment and bottles, mixing what looked like a magic potion with water and depositing bottles and teats in it. He then got the can of powdered milk, and made up some formula. Harvest meanwhile was getting so hot with all the crying, that Flora had taken off her cardigan and woollen bootees to try and calm her down.

Finally, thank heavens, the warmed formula was ready. After one last shake of the bottle to make sure it was properly mixed, and then pouring a drop on the back of his hand to test it wasn't too hot, Richard held it out at last to Harvest who grabbed at it hungrily and began to suck furiously.

'You'd better sit down, and take this towel with you. Poor little thing's so hungry, she's gulping it down so there's likely to be a lot of wind.'

'Wind,' Flora's face crumpled, 'yikes, what do you do about that?'

'You wind her of course. Don't worry, when she's finished I'll show you.'

'What's the hanky for?'

'Well,' Richard hesitated, 'there might be a bit of sick as well.'

'Oh yuck, babies are so . . . yucky aren't they?'

Richard chuckled as he watched Harvest clutching Flora's sleeve in sheer delight as the warm milk disappeared. 'They're not yucky all the time but they do have their moments. Here,' he sat the baby up on Flora's lap and showed her how to rub her back. 'There, that's how you wind them. That's right, now pat her a bit between the shoulders.'

'What's the point of all this back rubbing?'

'You'll see.' Richard sat back. 'And it shouldn't take too long by the looks of the pink face and the crossed eyes on that baby.'

Suddenly, an enormous burp rang through the air. Flora's eyes were wide with shock. 'Heavens, was that meant to happen?'

'Yup, that's what all the rubbing was about. See how much happier she looks? Better out than in, is what I always say.'

'Well, you're no young lady are you Harvest? What an extraordinary noise to come from someone so small.'

In a moment, Flora had collapsed in giggles. Whether it was joy at having stopped the baby crying or relief at having been able to do something right for Harvest, she didn't know, but Flora finally felt relaxed and was endlessly grateful that Richard had known exactly what to do.

'Thank you Richard,' she blurted out once she had recovered.

'For what?'

'For being the most excellent surrogate father any baby could ever want. And for being here and helping me.'

As she said the words, Flora found herself holding her breath. There was something about the intimacy of the situation — two people alone together with no other sound than the crackling of the fire and the gurgling of the baby nestled in her lap — that was delicious but also too close for comfort.

She thought she saw a light shine in Richard's eyes which told her that had she gone on, he might well have moved across towards her and perhaps, just perhaps, kissed her. That must never happen. They were two people thrown into a highly emotional situation, looking after a tiny life. That mustn't sway things onto uncharted territory.

The memory of Damian and all the evil things he had done was far too clear in her mind to ever let her slip unguarded into another relationship. Just as surely as Flora's defences had come down, they shot up again.

Abruptly, she stood up, carefully placed the baby down on the rug and said distantly, 'I need to wash my hands, please excuse me, Richard.'

As she went, she was sure she saw a look of disappointment on Richard's strong features and that confirmed for her that she must never, never give him any cause for false hope.

6

Richard had never seen Flora in her
pyjamas before but, he thought as he
hesitated outside her bedroom on the
way to bed, there was a first time for
everything in any relationship. They had
washed up together after dinner, and
put another two logs on the fire and
shut it down so that it would tick over
until morning. That warmth was
nothing to the glow he felt inside at
doing these simple night time chores
with Flora. Often over the years, they
had had great long conversations, yet
they could also be completely silent,
going about their business, totally
content with each other.

But always there had been the point
where they had said goodbye, each
gone back to their own houses and
finished the day alone. Without fail, he
had felt a dip in his mood at that point.

Every time she left, the house felt colder without her, thoroughly empty without her gentle presence.

This evening was different. For the first time, they were finishing the day together, and Richard was delighted to have carried out small domestic chores finishing the day in her company.

Normally, he did the washing up like a robot. But today, standing there drying up whilst she washed had been a pleasure. She was the only woman he knew who could look gorgeous with her arms up to the elbows in soap suds. Seeing her, knowing they would soon be sleeping under the same roof had caused a lightness in his chest which could only be described as euphoria. It didn't matter that it was still snowing outside, or that they had used half the logs already, it was of no consequence that they were in danger of being snowed in for days.

What did it matter if he had Flora all to himself? He liked looking after her. She was feisty and independent, but there was a vulnerability somehow, and sometimes a sadness when she referred to the past that he wanted to know more about.

Just once, she had mentioned the name of her former fiancé to him, Damian. The word had stuck in her throat. Whatever that guy had done to her, it had caused deep scars. And most of all, it had stopped her trusting another man. Richard could always detect the drawbridge being drawn up as soon as he tried to get closer to her.

Maybe, he thought, as he made the fire up for the night, being flung together in this situation, she might feel able to confide in him. He had given the fire one last rake, before going to the kitchen and stopping her doing anything more that night.

'We'd better think about turning in. You're beginning to look tired.'

'I am actually.' She had turned the back of her hand to stifle her yawn in a way that he found incredibly attractive. Ladylike, vulnerable, quirky. As he watched her follow it with a stretch, Richard thought for the thousandth time how Flora looked like a gorgeous Persian cat — or rather kitten, for she had childlike features, perfectly symmetrical with wide eyes.

He stopped himself from staring at her and said gruffly, 'Come on, you mustn't do any more work today. I insist. As a new and inexperienced mother, I give you top marks for your first day in training and permission to go up to bed and get some rest. You'll need it, Harvest will keep you busy enough tomorrow.'

'Thank you.' She'd finished her stretch, and was taking off her apron. 'You have been the most excellent teacher. Coming from a large family definitely has its bonuses. I couldn't have done it without you.'

Richard looked embarrassed. 'Come on, let's go and sort out the sleeping arrangements.'

It was decided that Flora should have Megan and Ryan's old bedroom.

Richard had noticed that Flora had placed a wedding photograph of Megan and Ryan face down on the chest of drawers. Flora and Megan hadn't been close but for now, it was much better that Flora live in the present.

The past was tinged with sadness at Megan's passing and the future held so many uncertainties. The present was full of warmth, cups of cocoa, and baby Harvest's gentle snoring. Besides, the present was where Richard felt comfortable. Tomorrow, they would be here, getting to know each other better than ever before. He couldn't contemplate the snow melting — and things getting back to normal didn't bear thinking about.

He had put his things in the small spare bedroom. 'Are you sure you'll be all right in here?' Flora asked. 'That bed barely looks big enough for someone over six foot and the ceiling's low. What if you knock yourself out and the baby starts crying with you out cold on the floor?'

'I'll be fine, there's more than enough room. Besides, here I can hear Harvest if she cries in the night and I don't mind getting up to her.'

'Why would she cry in the night? She's snoring like an old man. She's been fed and watered, I thought we'd both get a lie in tomorrow.'

Richard shook his head. 'You've got so much to learn. Who knows what wakes them up? Babies are the most complex of creatures, sometimes even they don't know why they're unsettled. The only thing you can do if they wake up is try every possible remedy. You change them, feed them, and if all else fails, pace up and down with them.'

'In the middle of the night, when it's freezing cold?' Flora shivered, drew her cardigan more closely around her slender frame and glanced at the snowflakes outside the window.

'Don't look so worried Flora. It's your first night in charge of Harvest so I'm happy to do the honours if she does wake up.'

99

A look of seriousness came over Flora's face. 'My first night in charge; that sounds terribly official. You do know this is just a trial and I don't think I can take charge of Harvest for ever, don't you, Richard?'

'Let's just live in the moment and not try and work out the next twenty years overnight. You'll sleep much better that way.'

She had gone off and he could hear her padding about in the bathroom. His room was warm, as the chimney from the stove ran through his room, and he chided himself for not offering this room to Flora. As soon as he had got his pyjama pants and t-shirt on, he resolved to go and offer to swap with her as he heard her go back to the main bedroom.

He stood outside the door now but hesitated. The last thing he wanted was to worry her into thinking he wanted something more. The two of them were alone under this roof together and they had shared domestic intimacy including tending to baby Harvest, making it feel as if they were a family.

As he felt the floorboards against his bare feet, the coldness didn't worry him, but he realised he did want something more, desperately.

The woman behind that door was so sweet when she tried to be strong. If only this was their bedroom, the bedroom they shared. If only they were partners, husband and wife, if only.

He heard Flora moving around inside and shook his head vigorously to get some sense into it. *Don't be stupid Richard Cross. Don't make any sort of move which might scare her however much you need and want her. You could spoil everything.*

He knocked.

'Yes?' she called and opened the door. It took his breath away. Long blonde hair, newly brushed, cascaded around her shoulders. She wore cream silk pants, a camisole with lace bodice and a wraparound angora cardigan of mint green. She looked like a beautifully iced wedding cake. The sweetness of lily of the valley body cream wafted from her like a spring garden at dawn.

He was tongue tied and had to clear his throat to make the words come out. 'I just wanted to check you had everything you needed. I . . . ' It was difficult to focus on what he was saying with those forget-me-not blue eyes looking up at him. 'I feel a bit bad . . . I think I chose the warmest room.'

Her smile, and the fact that she gently touched his arm, gave him butterflies somewhere deep in his stomach. 'I'm as warm as toast. Thank you so much for everything you've done for us both. See you tomorrow.'

In a second the moment had passed and he stood alone, her door closed and his feet like frozen blocks of ice. He went off thoroughly lonely, and worst of all, feeling like a complete fool.

★　★　★

By the time Flora was washed and dressed the next morning, and coming down the stairs, the smell of toast and coffee already greeted her nostrils on the morning air.

'You're up early,' she said as Richard bustled in with a tray of marmalade, jam and marmite.

'That's right, Harvest and I were up early.' The baby sat up at the table in her high chair happily sucking a teething ring. 'In fact we were up at two, then again at four and finally at six. At which point we decided, we might as well stay up to greet the dawn.'

'Oh Richard, I'm so sorry, I had no idea. I slept like a log.'

'No worries,' he said breezily pouring steaming coffee and setting down plates with boiled eggs. 'I must have an internal clock which responds to the noise of babies waking. It's coming from a large family. We always had tons of cousins staying with us. I can wake up fully but then get back to sleep straight away, although once it's past six in the morning I'm happy just to potter around. It doesn't matter as I'm not at work. I can have a doze this afternoon if I want. The fire stayed in all night by the way, I just gave it a prod and it leapt into life.'

'It is warm down here. I haven't taken notice of what's happening outside except to see it's stopped snowing thank goodness.'

'I think it's going to brighten up. There was blue sky first thing.'

'Do you think it'll melt today?'

'No, not in a day,' Richard said, slicing the top off his egg. 'There's too much of it and last night was well below freezing.'

A worried look passed over Flora's face. Getting anxious over phoning the airline and asking them what the position was on flights to New York would be pointless if the snow was too deep to drive back to the airport.

Besides, she thought as she looked at Harvest who was vigorously shaking a rattle, it was so peaceful and cosy here.

Flora knew this situation was temporary but it was a welcome rest from making decisions and plans. The disappointment about not getting to New York on schedule had hit her hard but she'd phoned the Hughes-Renton Museum on her mobile and they too had a big freeze in Brooklyn. It was so snowy in New York people were staying indoors.

She had told the museum about her situation and the sudden and unexpected death in the family and they had been incredibly understanding. All the more reason that she wanted eventually to go and join them; they would be nice people to work for.

Richard was such pleasant company, and Flora realised that this enforced rest had in an odd way come at a good time. For the past few months so much of her time had been spent rushing around decorating, she'd been on a crazy treadmill. A week or so delay so that she would be fresh when she did get to New York was a good thing.

Flora buttered a slice of toast, and looked at Harvest. Sadness shot through her like a thorn. What on earth was to happen to Harvest? The baby looked at Flora, holding out her little hand, the fingers spread like a starfish, so innocent of anything as complicated as the future. Flora held out her hand and Harvest clutched it, the soft chubby fingers curling around with a surprising strength. Flora found a lump come to her throat.

It was so much easier to look at Richard who was rugged and handsome and much more relaxed than normal. He wore a cream coloured polo neck. His skin, tanned from his recent holiday, exuded the odd tang of aftershave. Every now and then, as they chatted he would rake his hands through his hair and dishevel it so that the light caught the brown and blonde streaks making him look like a young Robert Redford.

There was nothing complicated about

Richard. He took life in his stride making decisions easily. Time spent with him was untroubled. Even the baby, thought Flora, seemed to warm to him, often holding out her arms for him to chuck her under the chin.

'When will the little 'un need some breakfast?' Flora wondered.

'Good point. She's ready now if you want to sort out a bottle.'

'Will do.' Flora took the breakfast things into the kitchen. She was becoming a dab hand at making up the milk, sterilising bottles and testing the temperature on the back of her hand.

Flora settled down in the sofa. As she cradled Harvest in her arm and she grabbed the bottle there was an unexpected ring at the doorbell.

'I'll go.' Richard got up. Voices from the front door filtered through to where Flora sat in the lounge.

'Good morning, I'm your neighbour, Nate Campbell. I hope you don't mind me calling.'

'Certainly not.' Richard came into

the lounge with a young man, tall and commanding with what Flora could only describe as 'presence'. This was Ryan's old friend whom Mr. Greig had mentioned as being a wealthy property developer. He was doubtless the same age as Ryan but seemed older in his bearing, with a swagger born of extreme wealth gained early on.

Nate strode over to her chair saying, 'Don't get up, you have your hands full. Ah, Harvest, thank heaven our little girl is okay. Miss Canning — Flora, can I call you that? Mr. Greig phoned me to say you were here. I only use my cottage for holidays. I've been down seeing family. I'm so sorry. The loss of Megan and Ryan was a great blow to their friends,' Nate said smoothly.

'Yes,' replied Flora, 'so tragic and so unexpected. Mr Greig told us about you. You were at school with Ryan.'

Richard had followed Nate Campbell into the room and offered him a coffee. It may have been Flora's imagination but she thought she detected an edge to

Richard's voice, Nate Campbell was good looking in an over-polished way and he fixed her in a direct, almost impertinent way. She wasn't surprised when Richard got the coffee and came back quickly.

'That's right, Ryan and I were as thick as thieves at school. Both of us came from the same council estate. Ryan was the dreamy eco-minded one, keener on saving the planet than anything. I'm afraid I was the more ruthless one, I even had a little business going while we were at school, selling t-shirts. I used to get them printed with the names of local bands.

'My business spiralled from there, I bought a market stall, then a shop, and then a whole string of shops. One thing lead to another and I eventually managed to invest in property in Wales before it became desirable. I've got a pretty good portfolio behind me now. I've spread far and wide — London, Europe, the States.'

'Mr Greig told us something about

you.' Richard pointedly sat down on the small sofa next to Flora even though there were spare chairs.

'All good, I hope.' Nate didn't look at Richard, keeping his gaze on Flora.

'He said you had some sort of interest in Harvest,' Richard pursued.

'I don't know if I'd quite put it like that,' replied Nate Campbell, 'that makes her sound like a commodity. But I've followed her progress carefully. I'd have liked children of my own, but unfortunately my business interests have never allowed me much room for a wife, let alone children. Lots of girlfriends have come my way, but they soon get fed up if you spend most of your life conducting business. I suppose I've looked on Harvest as being a bit of a surrogate child for me. You know of course that she's my goddaughter?'

Richard and Flora glanced at one another. 'No,' said Flora, 'we didn't know. You see Megan was younger than me and not my full sister but a half sister. We'd lost touch, I didn't even know about Harvest until the hospital phoned me.'

'Gosh, that's rough. Little Harvest's the silver lining that every cloud's meant to have though isn't she? I envied Ryan you know. Harvest's such a lovely kid, and she's bright. That's partly what I came here about. I don't know if anyone told you but Ryan and I had a sort of agreement.'

'What agreement was that?' asked Richard flatly.

'Well, neither Ryan nor I had much education. I made good despite my lack of learning. And Ryan never wanted more than what he had. So he was happy. He was good with his hands, he did up this cottage. I used to tell him to slow down. He was working day and night but he said it was worth all the effort for Megan and Harvest. I guess he was right in the end.

'But I've always had bigger ambitions. I told him he should have too, for Harvest. I used to say to him over a beer, 'Think what we could have been, you and I, if we'd had an education.' I can always see the possibility of more.

'So I offered him a gift. As Harvest's godfather, I said I'd pay for her to go to private school. Then she'd have as much chance as all those stuck up guys I have to deal with who've had it handed to them on a plate. With a private education, and beauty as well as brains — which I can see your family has in spadefuls,' Nate looked appreciatively at Flora, making her blush, 'goodness knows what Harvest could achieve.'

Flora made polite noises, but she could see Richard's foot tapping the floor in a way which meant he was annoyed. She'd seen him do the same thing when he'd been dealing with difficult clients at work. Flora steered the conversation away from Harvest and on to more general areas, the weather, Nate Campbell's business. It turned out that part of Nate's property portfolio was an apartment in Brooklyn.

'Do you know Brooklyn?' he asked, looking fascinated and cutting Richard out of the conversation. 'I chose that area because it's up and coming. It's one of those poor areas right next door to an upmarket area. It's ripe for the plucking.'

Briefly, Flora told him about the museum and her proposed job but said that everything was temporarily on hold now that she had Harvest to consider. It was nearly lunch time by the time Nate Campbell left. Richard's jaw looked hard set as he closed the door and strode back into the lounge.

'He seems like a determined guy. You weren't very chatty, is there something wrong?' said Flora after she had placed Harvest down on a rug with some toys.

'I don't much like his sort, pushy and ambitious. He may have come from a humble background but that doesn't mean he has to spend his time telling everyone how successful he is.'

'I don't think he was doing that, I

think he just wanted to make conversation and steer me away from thinking about Megan. He's an interesting guy though and he gave me a few useful addresses in Brooklyn.'

'Hmm. I wasn't crazy about the way he was trying to muscle in on Harvest and her future. Those decisions are for you to make Flora, you're her family now.'

'True, but I wouldn't want to deny her any chances in life, and I'd want to do what Megan and Ryan wanted as much as possible. Nate's her godfather after all and he was far closer to Ryan and Megan than I am. I wonder in some ways why Megan didn't name him in her will as the one to look after Harvest.'

'Do you?'

'Yes.'

'Why? Your stepsister had her head very much screwed on there Flora. Megan may have been flighty and new-ageish but it strikes me she could see that Nate Campbell is self-centred.

He thinks money can buy everything people need. He obviously thinks money is the most important thing in everyone's lives.

'Did you see the car in his driveway? It's a red Porsche, a status symbol if ever I saw one. He's obviously very proud of it, too — he's cleaned all the snow off. In fact, I wonder if the reason your stepsister was so intent on telling Dr Greig her last wishes was because she feared that Nate Campbell might otherwise have too great an influence over Harvest. Perhaps Nate was a bit domineering towards Ryan. From all you've said about him he sounds like a simple guy.'

'He was,' mused Flora. 'Quiet and simple and likable. Maybe you're right. But, a private school would be wonderful for Harvest.'

Richard said gruffly, 'I'm going outside to get more wood.'

Moments later, washing up the breakfast things, Flora was intrigued to see Richard wielding a large axe he had found next to the woodpile. He was attacking logs with a fervour bordering on anger. Could he be jealous? Flora shook the idea out of her head. That was ridiculous, what had he to be jealous about? And yet, he seemed to be attacking that log with more ferocity than necessary.

7

That afternoon, the snow stopped, and the sun came out with a vengeance. Richard seemed in a lighter frame of mind having worked out some of his energy on the logs that he'd stacked up in the fireplace. 'Why don't we put a casserole on the stove and get out and enjoy this weather?'

Once it was agreed, Flora chopped vegetables, fried onions and chicken and put everything on the stove to braise. Meanwhile, Richard had found Harvest's warm clothes and wrapped her up ready for their adventure. The three of them set off around the back of the house and into the woods where the sun made the snow sparkle like diamonds.

Richard set Harvest on his shoulders, and she seemed delighted to be so high, giggling as he tramped through the trees with her pretending to be a horse while Flora chased them.

'Crikey I'm exhausted,' he said, coming into step beside Flora. 'Isn't this the most glorious weather? Just like a scene on a Christmas card.'

'I thought Wales would be dingy and much too dull for me to want to paint it. But I think Megan and Ryan really discovered something when they chose this place. The light's clear, not suffused with smog like it is in the city. And seeing those birds wheeling up ahead, they make such lovely silhouettes against the sky. I feel really inspired. If you can cope with looking after Harvest when we get back, I might do some sketches.'

'Sure,' he said. 'After running about, I really need to sit down, put my feet up and drop off.' He'd lifted Harvest off his shoulders and cradled her in his arms. 'And, if I'm not mistaken, Harvest is about to nod off too.'

He was right. When they got back to the cottage, Harvest's eyes had started to close.

'It won't be long now,' he said. 'You go out and do your sketching.'

'Oh good, I don't feel quite so guilty going off and leaving you holding the baby if you're both ready for a doze.' She grabbed her stuff from the car. 'There'll be two hours of this light left.'

Richard waved her away. 'You still need your freedom, we all do. Take care, don't go far, and don't get cold.'

As she took her bag of sketching material and waved him goodbye, she couldn't help reflecting how she always felt happier with Richard. She brushed the snow off a fallen log, sat down and took out her pad of paper and charcoal. She sketched the trees with their snowy icing and marvelled at the way the late afternoon sunbeams created dramatic shadows.

As she sketched, the charcoal dancing across the paper, something brought her up short, stopping her hand in mid flow. The snow was like a huge bridal dress which had fallen over the ground.

It made her think of the white silk

wedding dress she had tried on when she was convinced all those years ago that Damian and she were going to get married and be the happy couple. In the silence of the snow, the memories came flooding back. Her belief in him had been unshakeable. On the odd occasion when her friends had remarked upon how much money Damian spent, she had defended him.

Chloe, Flora's friend, had remarked one day, 'But surely, he's a junior architect, he's not a partner or anything Flora. I'm just amazed at how much they pay him, he's very lucky to have got such a wonderful job.'

Four of them had gone out to lunch and Damian had ordered the most expensive wine on the menu — fifty pounds a bottle — but he insisted it was worth it and they wouldn't regret it. 'Don't worry,' he'd urged Flora when she'd tried to signal to him with her eyes that their friends were embarrassed by such conspicuous expenditure. 'I got a bonus this month for those plans I did for the housing estate. This meal's on me.'

Flora had smiled uneasily, but Damian was a terrific architect and such a likeable person. He had strings of friends. The lads he played rugby with all seemed to think he was a great guy. His mobile never stopped ringing with invitations.

Besides, Damian was the one who had suggested they start saving for a place for when they were married and he was the one who put the first money into a joint account they set up. He was good at figures and he and Flora had sat down and he had worked out precisely how much it was fair for each of them to put in based on their earnings. Flora was delighted to see how committed Damian was to their future. Soon, she had thought, soon she would show her stepfather Peter what a good man Damian was. True, he spent a fair bit but he earned lots and saved too.

They'd chosen a wonderful little

house. It was off plan, on a totally new development. Damian had calculated that they would be able to afford the deposit in the year it would take for the land to be cleared and the houses to be completed.

During that year, Flora thought of nothing else apart from how happy they were going to be in the house. She was alarmed when Damian had bought a new car, but said that work had given him an interest free loan and it was only a matter of paying a small amount off each month. They had wanted him to look professional when he went to see clients so it suited them. Flora had never been interested in the trappings of wealth. She saw the car as a burden as it always needed something new doing to it each month, or Damian would decide to put in some new gadget.

Still, he was working hard, and entertaining clients even during the evenings so Flora didn't doubt that he was well thought of at work.

It was only her friends, like Chloe, who would comment about Damian's buying another new suit or watch and look at Flora with a quizzical expression. But Flora trusted Damian. That was part of what being in love was all about.

All this Flora had been remembering with bitterness as she sketched the beautiful woodland scene. What had made her even think of Damian? Of course it was the snow being bridal white. Thank heavens she had never married Damian. He had still done her damage but it would have been worse if they had been married. And far, far worse if they had had a baby.

At that time, when she was so happy with Damian, Flora remembered that she had thought about the joy of having a baby with him. She had looked at couples with young children and thought how complete they were. She had never been particularly maternal but being in love with Damian, dreaming of their own family had begun to appeal to her.

As she thought about it now, a shiver ran through her bones. She looked down at her paper and realised she had completed half a dozen sketches. They were good ones too. One day she would get her paints and turn them into a canvas, but now it was time to go back to the cottage.

As she was gathering her things together she saw a figure in the distance and thought it was Richard. Joy went through her at the thought of him until she realised that the figure didn't have his rolling, relaxed way of walking. This was someone in a hurry. Also Richard would never have been irresponsible enough to leave Harvest on her own. As the figure came closer, Flora realised it was Nate Campbell, wearing the latest skiing gear and a pair of expensive RayBan sunglasses. He waved and shouted, 'Hi!'

'Hi,' she called back. 'I was just packing up.'

'Sketching were you?' he asked.

'That's nice. You don't often see snow like this, particularly when no one's stepped in it. Richard around?'

'Yes,' she replied, wondering why he was asking. 'Well, he's back at the cottage actually. He and Harvest are taking a nap.'

'Great, that means you and I can have a chat, just the two of us, about Harvest. After all, he isn't related to her in any way, is he? Not even connected to her in the way I am, being her godfather.'

'No,' she replied whilst thinking to herself, but he is fantastic with her and has her best interests at heart. In fact, he always puts other people before himself — she was sure that could not be said of Nate Campbell.

As they started to walk, she got the feeling Nate was going slowly to keep her out alone for as long as possible. She didn't mind hearing what he had to say, but wondered why he didn't want Richard around.

'You know Flora, I could do an awful

lot for Harvest. I don't have any children of my own, may never have. But I've done well in life and I like that little kid. Kids are expensive. It's not just education they need. There's so much I'd planned to give her. I'd talked to Ryan about giving her a horse when she got older. Girls love horses and I promised Ryan he could stable a horse in the paddock at the back of my cottage. I only really use the cottage for the odd break.'

'Did you ask Megan?' Flora turned her piercing blue eyes on Nate.

But he brushed off her comment. 'I didn't see as much of Megan as I saw of Ryan. He and I used to have loads of mates down at football. But he was keen to take me up on any offer to help Harvest, he wasn't proud about things where his daughter was concerned. All I want to say, Flora, is that I hope you won't be too proud either. I have a lot of time on my hands nowadays. I've made a lot of dosh and now I want to spend it. I was hoping to spend it on

Harvest. She's going to be a lucky little girl who won't have to want for anything.'

Flora found herself uneasy in his presence. She suspected that his pushiness was useful in business but it worried her. He was making a fantastic offer, after all. Who was she to turn down opportunities for Harvest, an orphan who needed as much help as she could get? Still, Flora shivered. Taking money from someone made you beholden to them. Money meant power and she wasn't sure she wanted Nate Campbell having any power over Harvest or over herself.

She stopped and looked directly at him. They were in sight of the cottage and it made her uneasy to think Richard might see them alone. She felt he had no time for Nate and wished he wasn't here. The failing light gave Nate's good looking dark features a sinister edge.

'Nate,' she asked bravely, 'what's in this for you?'

'My my,' he replied, a smile breaking out on his lips which didn't reach his eyes. 'You should have gone into business. You don't mind calling a spade a spade do you? I don't usually lay all my cards on the table Flora, but you've asked a direct question so I'll answer it. Megan and I . . . your stepsister . . . Well, nothing came of it, but I went out with her before she started seeing Ryan. I won't beat around the bush, I was madly in love with her. Quite frankly, she was far too good for Ryan.

'Not that he wasn't a great guy, he was my friend. But he was a dreamer. He used to make big plans but never carried them out. He ended up a carpenter with next to no money because that's what suited him.

'I don't know why Megan chose him instead of me apart from the fact that she was a dreamer too. Women have strange notions about what they want. She had these crazy ideas about wedded bliss and turning that little

128

cottage into a smallholding. She wanted chickens and goats and was happy to wade around in Wellington boots and an old overcoat.

'What a waste! She was a fantastic looking girl who should have been holidaying in the Caribbean on a yacht, staying in the best hotels, going to smart parties dressed in designer gear. I could have given her all that but she chose dorky old Ryan.

'Why, I'll never know. Anyway, when I came back here, I couldn't keep away from her. She was like a magnet. Just knowing she was here drew me back. That's why I've kept the cottage for so long. It doesn't suit my lifestyle being out here in the middle of nowhere, but wanting to see Megan always brought me back.

'When she announced she was pregnant, it really stung me. The thing is, I've been out with loads of women but never wanted to marry any of them apart from Megan. But she didn't choose me. I never understood it, but that's life. When I saw Harvest though, I felt there was a little bit of hope. Ryan and Megan didn't have two beans to rub together, they were dirt poor. They couldn't give her a proper start in life. But I could and I wanted to.

'She was the only bit of Megan I could have. My money can do that child some real good if only you'd agree, Flora. If you take Harvest on, you'll be bringing her up alone, as a single mother. I could make a huge difference.'

There was a silence where Nate was waiting for an answer. She could see the need to possess something of Megan burning in his eyes. Suddenly Flora felt sorry for him.

Although he was still young, good looking and wealthy, yet there was an emptiness about him which it was crushingly sad to see. He was so used to getting everything he wanted but the one thing he had really wanted, the woman he had set his heart on, had married someone else.

'Don't you see, Flora . . .' He stood in front of her, taking her by the shoulders, desperation in his eyes. 'I want to help you to look after Harvest. I've got more money than I know what to do with. I'm not the marrying kind. I'm married to my work. Making money gives me a kick, it's an addiction and I'm darned good at it. But it doesn't make me feel good inside. Helping Harvest is one of the few things which does make me feel good inside.

'If I could see her when she's older doing well in life, beautiful like Megan, but well educated with a fantastic career . . . Well, that would actually be worth more than the money I have in all my bank accounts. With my help, she could be a lawyer, a doctor, the sky's the limit. I want to be part of that.' He dropped his arms, waiting for Flora's answer.

She felt swamped. When she'd come to Wales to see Harvest, she'd never expected to face these dilemmas. Nate

Campbell was offering a fantastic opportunity. And yet it didn't seem right. Nate wasn't Harvest's father however much he had loved her mother. He was a strong, pushy, commanding man. If Flora accepted his money would she not be exposing Harvest to pressure from him later in life?

As she stood, not knowing where to turn, she looked at the cottage and saw a light go on. Richard would be wondering where she was. Frozen to the core, she couldn't give Nate an answer. She turned blue eyes upon him. 'I've got to go. Richard will think I've got lost.'

'Will you let me help Harvest?'

'I can't tell you right now. I have to think.'

As she walked away his voice carried after her on the icy air. 'Think very hard Flora. This is a once in a lifetime offer. I need an answer soon.'

His words hung like frost on the night air as Flora turned and watched him stomp off. For a moment she was rooted to the spot.

Demanding, domineering, impatient, overbearing — Nate Campbell was all of those and more. She could well understand why Megan had chosen Ryan with his gentle ways over him. She ran back indoors and as she stood in the hallway of the cottage pulling her boots off, she realised her heart was pounding fit to burst.

Richard opened the door from the lounge and she ran, for the first time ever, into the warmth of his arms.

'What on earth has happened?' he said, enfolding her, holding her tight.

'I . . .' Flora didn't know what to say. She was the one who had to take responsibility for Harvest. She was the one who had to decide whether to say yes or no to all that money. She knew what Richard would say. He didn't like Nate Campbell. He had recognised ruthlessness and raw power and would surely tell her to turn down the money. And yet she knew that Nate was right when he said his offer was a once in a lifetime chance. She was confused, dizzy, freezing cold.

'I . . . got a bit lost. I'm sorry, I went beyond where we walked today and I thought I might not find the cottage again. It was scary and dark. I'm so pleased to be back inside.'

Richard held her. She felt protected in his arms, but she tore herself away and held him at arm's length. The feeling of being held by a man was wonderful, but men were trouble. She'd only been thinking a short while ago how Damian had let her down and now she'd had to deal with Nate and his ultimatum. Men were just bad news.

Disappointment was plain on Richard's handsome features. He looked as if he would be happy to hold her in his arms forever. His chocolate brown eyes gave her a melting look as he lead her to the sofa, tucking a blanket around her. A low sigh came from his soft lips as he said, 'Don't worry. You're home safely now. I'll get you a cup of cocoa.'

8

That night, Richard lay in bed listening to Flora moving about. His chest was tight with rage and sadness. It had been a mistake coming here. He shouldn't have got involved. Except he knew he was involved, much more than he wanted to be because this afternoon he had had to admit to himself what he had known all along. That he had fallen fully, crazily, lastingly, hopelessly in love with Flora.

Years they'd known each other. All those times they'd spent together having fun, drinking wine, talking out each other's problems. All those moments had been a dress rehearsal for this one day. This day when Richard feared he might lose her.

Today had been worse than the day she had announced she was going to America, for he had always hoped maybe she would try it, decide she didn't like it and return. Or that he would go out there on holiday to see her and finally have the courage to tell her he couldn't live without her. He would have been prepared to move to America to be with her. Let's be honest, he thought smiling wryly, he would have gone to the moon to be with Flora.

But today was the worst day of his life. When he had woken from his nap, the sun was long gone and he only then realised how late it was. Flora should have been back ages before, and he'd started to get worried. The baby was asleep and much as he had hated to leave her on her own, he was sure Harvest would be okay while he popped outside the cottage and looked back into the woods to see if he could spot Flora returning.

Richard had grabbed a jacket and shot out of the cottage. The first thing he saw had been a set of large, male footprints which weren't his own.

Prickles of concern had spiked the back of his neck and his heart began to race. As his eyes followed the path they made, he caught the sight of two figures in the near distance.

Flora and Nate Campbell. Nate had his hands on her shoulders, as if they had just embraced. Richard felt sick in his stomach. He had stopped dead in his tracks and hidden behind the wall of the cottage. The bright still night and the covering of snow seemed to carry the sound of their words on the crisp cold air. Once the blood had stopped thumping in Richard's head, he had then heard very clearly what the raised voices were saying, first Flora's, 'I can't tell you right now. I have to think.'

Then Nate Campbell's stern and insistent, 'Think very hard Flora. This is a once in a lifetime offer. I need an answer soon.'

At those words, Richard's world had imploded. He had felt as if he wanted to throw up. Slowly, moving like a cat, he had eased himself back towards the cottage, stepping in the footprints he had made before. No way did he want Flora to know what he had heard. She would be back soon and he had to compose himself before she got in.

What had it meant? They'd only just met but Richard had seen the look in Nate Campbell's eyes earlier in the day when he'd been talking to Flora. It was a look of hunger, a look of appreciation. Any man looking at Flora couldn't fail to acknowledge how gorgeous she was.

As Richard lay in bed, his mind churning over the events of the day, he chastised himself for bringing Flora here. If he was honest, he had hoped that once Flora had seen Harvest, she would have been unable to leave the baby. He had hoped that she would agree to look after the baby forever, and let him take her back home. He had wished that the baby would be a means to keep Flora in England and that just maybe he would be able to step in and take on a fathering role which might persuade her that he was a good man, different from the man who had wronged her. If he was honest, he had tried to use the baby as a means of making her accept him because he wanted her more than anything in the world.

And now it had backfired.

He couldn't sleep. He got up and pulled on his towelling robe. He went to the window and stared at the pit in the snow which had been worn by both his footsteps and those of Nate and Flora. What the hell was Nate thinking? He had everything. He could have any woman he wanted. And yet he seemed to have chosen Flora on the thinnest of acquaintances.

Richard raked his hands through his hair. He could see the attraction. She was beautiful, desirable, young enough to have children and become a trophy wife. He felt nauseous; the thought of her with that man made his stomach churn. And of course Nate had already stated that he wanted to have some control over Harvest — he was all about control — his words to Flora rang in Richard's ears again, 'This is a once in a lifetime offer. I need an answer soon.'

Nate was used to seeing something and buying it. He had seen Harvest and now she came as a package with Flora and he was doing his best to 'buy' a ready made family. Nate was too busy to go out and form proper relationships which took time and effort. He was trying to grab Flora when she was vulnerable and facing difficulties.

What woman wouldn't give in to a man like Nate? He said he had property in New York. He could give her everything she wanted. A nanny to look after Harvest when she was at the museum and a private education for Harvest. Who knew what he had proposed to Flora? Had he offered to help her become established as an artist? He had the money and he probably had the contacts to further her career. He could fulfil her dreams.

Richard pressed his forehead against

the glass pane. The coldness shot through his brow making his head ache. But it was nothing to the pain he felt at the thought of losing Flora.

He must do something to win her. But what? He wasn't wealthy, he wasn't connected, he couldn't whisk her off to New York and support her and Harvest without a job there. The worst thing was when he had tried to move their relationship to another footing, he had come up against a brick wall. She had occasionally mentioned a fiancé but it had all gone wrong. If only he could find out what had happened, then maybe he had a chance of persuading her that he wasn't like that.

But most of all he must get her away from Nate Campbell. He must take them back home where Flora wouldn't be under Nate's influence. Perhaps then, Richard could make her see sense, make her realise what a schemer Nate was. Once he had made the decision, he felt better.

He looked at his watch. It was the

middle of the night, but he had to speak to Mr Greig, the surgeon had been on night duty earlier in the week and probably was now. He grabbed his mobile, feeling as if he were standing on the edge of a precipice as he waited for the ringing tone to connect them. Finally, Mr Greig's tired voice answered.

'Richard Cross, yes of course, I remember you. You're Flora Canning's companion. How's Harvest?'

'She's doing great. It's Harvest I wanted to talk to you about. If Flora wanted to take her back to London could we do that, just for a few days?'

There was a moment's silence before Mr Greig said, 'Well, she's with you now, and if you left tomorrow morning and I'd known nothing about it then I couldn't have stopped you, could I?

'Frankly Mr Cross, the hospital is still inundated with patients. We've had a lot of elderly people in who've suffered from the cold. As long as you give me details of the address where you're taking the baby and a landline where I can contact you, I'd be only too pleased if you and Flora would look after her. She's much better off in a home environment for the time being.'

So that was it, settled. Now all he had to do was persuade Flora to take Harvest back home and out of Nate Campbell's grasp.

As he settled back into bed, he felt more in control. Nate Campbell wasn't the only guy who could hatch a plan. Richard would tell Flora he had been called back urgently to work. Hopefully it would be a simple job to persuade her that, with the hospital overloaded, it was best to take Harvest with them. With those thoughts calming him, he drifted into a heavy sleep.

* * *

Flora woke early next morning. She'd found herself tossing and turning, thinking about Nate Campbell's desire to shower Harvest with horses and payments for private schools. Was that a

143

good idea or not? Nate felt he could buy the little girl's love but wouldn't that risk spoiling her? And who was to say that his interest in the little girl would continue. He was just as likely to have some other hobby or business concern crop up on his radar and then he might forget about her all together.

The dilemma tormented Flora as she went about her morning routine. She opened the bathroom door and stepped into the passage, a towel wrapped around her, and bumped into Richard.

He stood there with just his jogging bottoms on and an expanse of wide tanned chest. She'd known he did a lot of sport, but she wasn't prepared for how muscular and toned his upper torso was. She was spellbound. It had been a long, long time since she had been this close to a man wearing practically nothing. He was fantastically good looking. Of course, she'd realised that many times before. She liked the way the squareness of his jawline gave him a noble, almost regal bearing

— but bare chested he looked devastating with the golden hairs on his chest matching his tan.

'I'm sorry.' She turned her eyes away, trying to focus on his words.

'Don't worry,' he answered, oblivious to the effect he was having on her. 'But there is something I wanted to ask you.'

'Can't it wait until breakfast?' She needed to run to the safety of her bedroom, and get dressed. It was far too edgy, him standing there and her in just a towel!

'I wish it could, but I've just had a call through on my mobile from work. The boss wants me back, right now.'

'Oh.'

'Yes, there are some problems at the firm which I audited recently. We have to go back to London — you, me and Harvest.'

'And Harvest?'

'That's right. I thought we could leave her at the hospital but I phoned Mr Greig and he said they simply don't have the capacity to take her back at the moment. It would be much better if we take her.'

'But isn't that a bit final, Richard? I am warming to her, it's true. But I still haven't decided if I can look after her. And what about New York? My place at the museum is still open.'

'Look Flora,' Richard gently placed his hands on each of her arms, and a thrill of adrenaline shot through her, like zooming up in a lift that's going really fast. It couldn't have been more different than when Nate Campbell had held her. That had made her feel trapped.

'The thing is if you leave Harvest at the hospital now, she'll get the barest of care. Things still aren't back to normal, power lines are down and all the services are stretched. She would be much better with us. Whatever decision you make, we can easily bring her back here. It's not so far away.'

At that point, Harvest woke. There were tiny baby noises and the sound of her batting the toys above her cradle.

Flora looked towards the nursery. She couldn't leave her yet. She wanted to be with her just a little longer.

'Okay Richard. You're right. It was good of you to bring me up here, and I can't stop you going back when you need to. I'll start packing our things.'

While Richard was in the bathroom, Flora dressed Harvest in a clean yellow jumpsuit with smiling bears over it. It only took her a moment to get her own things packed and in the hallway while Harvest was warm and contented in the lounge. As she placed her suitcase by the front door, she noticed a message pad and pen next to the telephone. It had troubled her that she would be going without telling Nate Campbell and letting him know where he could contact her.

Flora had had a chance to think things through — they always looked clearer in the morning. For her own part she didn't care if she never saw Nate Campbell again. But for Harvest's sake, she wanted to keep open the door to him as a possible benefactor. Adoption was one possible future for Harvest although even thinking of it made her blanch. If that was the future she chose for Harvest, it would be wrong of her to deny the child the expenditure Nate Campbell was willing to lavish on her.

Hastily, Flora penned a brief note including her contact details and slipped out of the cottage before Richard could find out. They hadn't mentioned Nate since he'd visited yesterday, both knowing that mention of him would cause trouble.

Everything was dark in Nate Campbell's cottage as Flora posted her note through his letterbox. She made it back to their cottage and slipped off her coat so Richard would never know she'd been out.

★ ★ ★

It wasn't long before she and Richard were packed into the car, with Harvest

148

in her car seat and the cottage locked up. Gradually they made their way down the lane and off towards the motorway.

On the drive back Harvest was as good as gold. Richard suggested they break their journey at a motorway service station. As they sat eating, the atmosphere between them was tense. After lengthy silences, Flora would try to break them and find as she opened her mouth that Richard started to speak too. Both of them could feel the unspoken questions in the air. But those questions, about what was to happen next, were too difficult even to ask, let alone to answer.

Suddenly, Flora blurted out, 'I phoned the museum from my mobile this morning. They say they'll keep the position open for another two weeks.'

'Right.' Richard, who normally had the appetite of a horse, pushed his food away.

'You don't seem very pleased for me.'

'I am, Flora, I am. I just . . . '

'Just what?'

'Hoped.' He swallowed hard. The waitress came and poured more coffee in their cups, making the moment even more painful, if that were possible.

'You mustn't hope Richard.' Flora looked down at her lap, anywhere other than at Richard.

'I'd hoped you might not go. There, I've said it.'

'Richard, you know I'd set my heart on it. There's a whole life waiting for me out there.'

'There's a life here for you. You're needed here.'

'Needed?' She so hoped that Richard didn't need her. He must find someone who could love him and appreciate all his wonderful qualities. Flora knew she was scarred by how Damian had treated her and she'd never wanted to mislead Richard.

'Needed by . . . ' Richard's expression told her that he was choosing his words carefully. 'Well, by Harvest of course. By Harvest.'

'I haven't made a final decision about her yet.' She pursed her lips. This was all so difficult. She looked over at Harvest whose face began to crinkle and threaten tears.

'Oh dear,' she said, grateful for a distraction. 'She's finished her bottle and still looks hungry. We didn't make up any fresh milk did we?'

'She's growing. Here, this might do the trick.' Richard got his fork and spooned some of the beans and their tomato sauce into a saucer and squished them till they were runny.

'You're not going to give her that are you?'

'This is about the age they start on solids but they have to be runny. Here, you try her with them.'

Flora picked up some of the mashed beans and offered them to Harvest. The baby turned her face away with a decidely rumpled expression. 'She doesn't like them.'

'It's a normal reaction to be scared of anything new. Look how you were the first time it was suggested you could look after a baby. And yet now that you have I think perhaps you're beginning to enjoy it a bit.'

'Maybe.'

'Sometimes we just have to be made to try something new. Here,' he said taking the spoon. He distracted Harvest's attention by rattling his keys above her head making her open her mouth and smile. Before she knew it, Richard had deposited some baked beans into her mouth. She blinked, looked startled then grinned. 'See,' said Richard proudly. 'If you don't try something you never know whether you really like it or not. And that goes for us, whatever age we are.

'Beans,' he smiled at Harvest as she finished her mouthful and went to stretch for the spoon. 'Beans.' Suddenly, Harvest opened her mouth, closed it quickly, opened and closed it like a fish in a bowl then said, 'Bees!'

'Richard,' Flora gasped, 'she's talking. She's trying to say beans. Oh my goodness! Her first word.'

'Well,' he smiled, 'nearly a word anyway.'

'It was. You're so clever, Richard, and so very good with her.'

His face became serious. 'Whatever happens Flora, I'll remember this moment for ever. It's almost like we were a fam — '

'Don't say it,' she stopped him. 'Please don't, Richard.'

'Why not? Why can't you ever imagine that you might have a husband and a family? I've never said this to you before, I've never questioned you about what happened with that fiancé of yours. But I think you owe it to me now. If you really are going to give all this up — give Harvest up, give England up and move away — at the very least you could tell me what happened so that I can make sense of it all when you're gone.'

Flora looked at Richard and felt herself melt. So few people knew what Damian had done to her. She was stupid to be taken in by all his lies and couldn't bear to tell anybody how she'd been so comprehensively duped.

With a deep sigh she said, 'Okay, Richard. I owe you an explanation.'

Her hand trembled. She saw him look at it, as if he was going to hold it but she willed him not too. Sympathy would have tipped her over the edge and that was the last thing she wanted to happen in public.

'Don't be kind to me, Richard,' she warned. 'I was such an idiotic fool over Damian, I don't deserve kindness.'

She held her own hand in a tight grip to stop it shaking as she told him the story she had hidden for so long.

'Damian was everything I ever wanted. Artistic, on my wavelength — or so I thought. I believed in love at first sight and trusted I'd found that with him. That first time he came to the school, I couldn't take my eyes off him. I was used to being surrounded by male teachers who were science geeks. Damian was a blast of fresh air. With his designer jackets and cool jeans, he laughed at the dusty academics with their beards and out of date courdoroy trousers. I was literally in seventh heaven when he asked me to marry him. Although my stepfather wasn't. Megan's father that was, Peter. He could see right through Damian. I just thought Peter was being authoritarian. I'd outgrown being told what to do by him. I thought my judgement was good but I was so wrong.

'It was Damian who said we should save for a flat. He suggested a joint bank account. I let him advise me on how much of my salary I should put in and he told me how much he was putting in. It was a lot. I didn't want clothes or jewellery or anything because I had him, so I put as much of my salary away every month as I could afford. It soon mounted up. In six months we'd saved thousands towards a deposit on the flat.

'The odd thing was that while Damian was saving he also seemed to be spending a lot. I never asked him what he earned. He convinced me he was good at budgeting and that his firm paid him regular bonuses. Damian certainly had the gift of the gab. And loads of friends — oh yes, he was Mr Popular. He always paid for rounds of drinks or footed the dinner bill when we were out. My friend Chloe tried to warn me it was too good to be true. But I simply wasn't interested.'

There was a pause. Flora could barely go on, this was the worst bit of her story. Richard stole his hand gently over the back of her hand. She closed her eyes feeling the comfort he gave her, opened them and went on.

'The house we had set our hearts on was nearly ready. It was new, we'd popped over to the site on a couple of occasions to check on progress with the builders. It was so exciting. We had saved up a great deal of money. I was so proud of us working together like that.

'On the day we were going to pay the deposit I found what had really been going on. After a year's saving it was going to be such a special day. Damian and I had agreed to meet to get a building society cheque to draw out the thousands of pounds we had saved to hand it over to the developers and secure our new house. I had chosen the colour scheme and curtains. In my head I'd already moved in. We agreed to meet in the pub and have a drink before we went to the Building Society.

'I waited but he didn't turn up. At first I thought a crisis at work or home must have blown up. I phoned his mobile, then I phoned his parents and his work. No one had a clue where he was. I even phoned the police. By then we were two hours late for our appointment and I was convinced he'd been in an accident.

'I finally went to the building society in case he had gone there first without me. That's when I learnt the truth. The girl behind the counter knew me well by then, I'd been in so many times to make deposits. She looked surprised to see me, especially when I asked her if Damian had been in. He had, two hours before. And he'd emptied the account of every penny. He'd made an arrangement days before to take the money in cash and produced signed documents, forging my name in order to steal all the money. All that I'd hoped for had disappeared. It was a sham. Damian was a sham. All along he'd used me to escape and build a new life that didn't involve me.

'I subsequently found he'd moved to Spain and left behind him huge credit card debts. All the restaurants we'd gone to, all the times he'd bought dinner for our friends, had been financed by a string of credit cards. He'd been putting the whole of his salary into the building society to make it appear as if he'd been saving when all along he'd been planning to make away with my money.

'He owed six months' rent on his flat and had done a moonlight flit. His car wasn't paid for, his clothes, nothing was. He was an illusion. I traced him to five different addresses in Spain. He constantly moved around. Then he disappeared. The police told me he'd undoubtedly changed his name. My life had come crashing down.

'Can you see now why I cannot bring myself to trust any man again?'

'We're not all like that.'

'You're right. But I can't bring myself to risk anything like that again.'

'I'm so sorry.' Richard squeezed her hand, but she pulled it away.

'Don't feel sorry for me. I was a fool, plain and simple.'

'No you weren't. I won't have you saying that. Con artists are clever, they choose good, trusting people. You mustn't blame yourself. Tons of women would have been taken in by someone that smooth.'

'Maybe, maybe not. I was an idiot, I got taken in. Now, I'm tired Richard. Please, can we get going?'

Flora picked up her things, gathering Harvest into her arms. Feeling the baby there, clinging on to her, gave her comfort. After all, it struck her all of a sudden, it is people who are important in life, not things and not money. You could recover from losing all your savings, and she had. But you couldn't recover from losing people, and gradually she realised Harvest was becoming more important to her.

* * *

When they got back to London, Flora phoned the people who were going to rent her house to ask if she could hang on to it for another week.

'They were very understanding,' she told Richard that night after they'd had a snack together. 'And thank goodness, now the snow is beginning to melt, maybe soon we'll all be back to normal.'

Richard didn't seem at all pleased to be going back to work the next morning but said he'd pop back during the day around some visits he had to make, to check if she and Harvest were okay.

'Don't go out unless you have to Flora. Although the snow looks like it's melting, underneath there's a solid layer of ice. I couldn't bear the thought of you going out with the baby and slipping, it's still treacherous. Are you sure you can manage the night on your own? It's a lot of responsibility being the only one around to get up and look after her.'

'Thanks Richard.' Flora stood at the door to wave him goodbye. 'But Harvest and I need this time together to help me choose what's best. These next few days will decide for me whether I give Harvest up to the authorities to get her looked after by someone else, or whether I take her on myself. Only by being alone together can I make that choice.'

'Okay,' Richard reluctantly accepted her decision. 'Remember though, call if you need me. I'm across the road and I'll have my mobile by my bed. I'm always there for you.'

She watched him disappear into his house, and felt as if there were an invisible silken ribbon which tied a part of her to Richard Cross and for once, she felt it tugging at her heart.

'Nonsense,' she said to herself shutting the door hastily, forgetting to give him her normal last wave. 'Nonsense. He's just a good friend.'

Yet the house seemed terribly empty without him. More so than normal.

Flora was surprised how well the next three days went. She and Harvest settled into a routine. Since Harvest had said her first word, Flora couldn't help trying to get her to say more. Like now, after a good lunch of pureed apple, she was showing Harvest some wooden jigsaw pieces in the shape of letters. She had even found herself looking at children's books on the internet and wondering which ones were best in helping a child to read.

Then she'd closed down the computer in disgust, amazed at herself for fantasising about bringing up a child, reminding herself that the plan she had been hatching for years was to be on her own with a bright new future in New York. Since she'd been looking after Harvest, her painting had gone to pot. She hadn't produced anything apart from those few sketches in the snow. Not having time to paint was like losing part of her identity.

Harshly she had told herself that that's what babies do, they take away your time and your freedom. As Flora wiped the jigsaw letters which had become sticky with apple puree she heard the doorbell and tucked Harvest up in the crook of her arm to go and open the front door.

9

An imposing figure with dark hair stood blocking out the light and stepped straight in without being invited. 'Hello Flora, I bet you weren't expecting me.' Nate Campbell's tones were silky with an edge which indicated he had important business to conduct.

'Now you're in, you'd better sit down,' Flora replied tersely. His presence filled the house, his eyes looking everywhere, taking an inventory of her house and possessions.

'Don't mind if I do. And a coffee'd be nice if you've got one on the go.'

'Of course,' said Flora between gritted teeth.

She took Harvest with her into the kitchen, putting her in her bouncy chair while she got out the mugs. Somehow, she didn't want to leave the baby alone with Nate.

Returning with a tray, Flora then brought Harvest in her chair and sat her in the corner as far from Nate as possible. She wished that Richard was here. Nate sat back, cross legged, one arm across his chest, the other stroking his chin, studying Flora. She felt like an exhibit under a microscope.

'So, this is where you and Harvest would live together if you decide to keep her, is it? In this tiny little house?'

'I haven't made my mind up yet, if that's what you mean.' No one was going to force her into a decision.

'That's what I'm here for today. I've been thinking. Solving problems, getting round obstacles is what makes me a good businessman. I've been pondering your dilemma and think I might have come up with a solution.'

Flora didn't answer. She made herself busy, pushing down the plunger on the cafetiere and pouring the coffee into mugs. 'It's good of you to spend your time solving other people's problems but actually I am capable of sorting myself out thank you.'

'Are you really?' His smile was cold and his eyes hard. 'But the trouble is there isn't just you to consider is there? There's Harvest to think of. Her future's at stake here. And you do seem to have something of a problem.'

Flora gave him a direct stare. She was in a flat spin about what decision to make. Nate Campbell had played a part in Harvest's life but there was no reason he should play a part in hers. If anyone had a right to do that, it was Richard. Sweet, caring Richard who always looked out for her. She felt a pang of guilt. He should be here now. Was it right of her not to involve him in this conversation when he had taken her to Wales and looked after her and Harvest so well?

Yet Richard wanted much more than she could give. A gaping emptiness settled in her heart. She waited for Nate Campbell with his smooth, in-control smirk to lay his cards on the table, and she couldn't help contrasting him with Richard.

Richard had no front, he didn't play games. Yet she couldn't trust him, nor any man after Damian. A knot settled in her stomach. She would have trusted Damian with her life and he had repaid her by cheating her and making a mockery of her devotion. That must never happen again.

Richard looked genuine but who was to say he couldn't turn like Damian had? Turn like a snake — surely every man was capable of that, weren't they? She looked at Nate. He might lay his cards on the table but he'd surely keep some up his sleeve.

'Your problem is,' Nate pronounced, oozing confidence, 'that you had a future all planned out which didn't include Harvest before she came along. A bolt out of the blue, she moved your life off its axis and sent it spinning. You're single, you don't have anyone to help you and you're not even sure you have the funds to look after her.'

Flora looked down. Her palms were sweating and she wiped them on her skirt. Everything he said was true. That's why she'd left her address with him. Poor Harvest had lost her parents, but Flora couldn't deny her any money which Nate might want to lavish on her.

'But I do. I've got more funds than I know what to do with. I want to help Harvest. And you, of course. That baby means something to me. She's the nearest I'll get to being a father. She needs a mother, and I don't have a wife. What's more, I'm not sure if I even want one. So, here's the deal.'

He sat forward in his chair, his eyes fixed with an intensity so strong they seemed to want to bore into her soul.

'You want to take up your post in New York and carry on with your art. I want you to keep Harvest and let me help with her schooling. So, I'll set you up rent free in the flat I have in New York, and I'll pay for her school. After all, she doesn't have to go to school in England. There are perfectly good private schools in New York state. I

know the Principal of this school . . . '
He opened his jacket and pulled out an expensive looking pamphlet with gold tooled lettering, The Oliveere School for Girls.

Flora ran her finger over the raised letters and flipped open the brochure. 'For girls who demonstrate superior intellectual and leadership potential.'

She read the words then glanced at Harvest who was blowing bubbles with the milk from her bottle and chuckling as they popped on her face.

Nate's voice pushed back into her consciousness, ' . . . and the Principal's agreed to put her name down. The school's so popular people put their child's name down before they're even born. I'll get a top-notch nanny in, to look after Harvest while you're at work. I quite fancy spending more time in New York myself. England's in such a state economically these days and I believe the recovery's going to start in the States so I've been seriously considering relocating there anyway.

'I won't get in your way. I'll just be there to see Harvest but I'll only do so when you're happy for me to. So, you see, keeping her need not cause you any inconvenience at all.'

Flora watched Harvest playing with her toes. Was she an inconvenience?

'It all makes perfect sense. You can go to New York and you can keep Harvest. You can live rent free and have all the help you need. You can have it all ways. You can have everything and so can Harvest.'

'I don't know what to say.'

'Just say yes. It makes perfect sense. I'm used to working out problems. You can do the best for Harvest and you can do the best for yourself. There is no downside.'

His words made sense, but why did Flora feel hollow? Why was there an uneasiness settling in her soul? 'I need some time to think about it.'

'I can't give you much time Flora. When I get an idea I don't hang around.' He got up, pulled his jacket closed, and pulled up the collar. 'You've got until tomorrow. I'm staying in a hotel up the road. I'll come back here after breakfast. This is a once only offer Flora. But just think, if you turn it down, you'll be turning down all Harvest's chances. She's had a lot of disaster in her young life. If you turn me down, you'll turn down one of the biggest chances she has. Could you live with that?'

With those words, he left. The silence closed in around her. Flora threw herself onto the sofa burying her face in her hands. He'd worked it all out, yet why had his offer tied her in knots? Why did it make her feel trapped? Money was the route to so many things. And yet, and yet, it left such a nasty taste in the mouth.

★ ★ ★

Richard stood at his bedroom window watching Nate Campbell leave.

He hadn't aimed to spy on Flora, he

171

had merely been checking on the weather, thinking that if it were nice, he would offer to take a walk with Flora and Harvest. That was when, with shocked disbelief, he'd seen Nate Campbell roll up in his ostentatious car, knock on Flora's door then push himself in like he owned the place. He was staggered to think that Flora must have given Nate her address.

The whole time Nate had been in the house with Flora, Richard had felt his anger rising. He wanted to burst in and demand to know what was going on. His guts had churned, his teeth had ground and his blood had boiled. Richard had known from the minute Nate Campbell had met Flora that the guy had been attracted to her. Not that she had encouraged him. But Nate was the sort of man who couldn't see fruit ripe on the tree and not pick it.

Richard watched Nate fold his tall body into the top of the range car that screamed wealth and possession, fire up the engine, and ease off down the road.

Richard dragged his fingers through his hair. What on earth was he to do? How could he get Flora to see that all the money in the world wouldn't buy her or Harvest happiness?

In an instant, not knowing what else to do, he grabbed his jacket, shot out of the house, jumped into his car and followed Nate. He caught up with him at the end of the road. When they got to the High Street, Richard saw Nate pull into the car park of the George Hotel. Richard parked and watched him get out of the car, smiling as he set off to the hotel with a confident swagger.

Richard banged his hand on the steering wheel. Damn him! Whatever that guy was up to, there was only one person who was going to benefit, and that was Nate Campbell. He went over and over in his head what he should do. Flora must be seeing Nate. What girl wouldn't be? Young, rich, handsome. How could he blame her for being swept off her feet?

He sat in the car brooding. Day

turned to evening, and still he sat. He knew what he was waiting for.

Flora was going to turn up any minute, dressed to the nines, to spend the evening with Nate. They'd go somewhere expensive. He'd wine and dine her then he'd start the process of stealing her away.

Nate already had a hold over her. After all he was Harvest's godfather. Although he suspected that was more Ryan's decision than Megan's. And Nate clearly wanted some control over the baby so he could fulfil his own ideas of making her into some high powered female version of himself.

The minutes ticked by. Richard could stand it no longer. He couldn't sit, waiting to spy on Flora like some weirdo stalker. She was an adult, she could make her own decisions.

He thrust the car into gear and screeched off. Yes, she had made her own decisions. That all men were like Damian and should be distrusted. She probably didn't trust Nate and yet she'd no doubt reasoned that at least she knew he was grasping and self-seeking from the start. At least a relationship with Nate Campbell would leave her and Harvest financially secure.

And, given what she had told him about how Damian had stolen all her savings, financial security would come high up on her list. Perhaps hooking up with Nate felt safer for her than falling for someone like himself. Someone dependable, safe, and boring who loved her with every fibre of his being.

Richard put the key in his front door and hesitated, turning briefly to look over to Flora's, Everything was quiet inside her house where he had spent so many wonderful hours. He wanted to run over, right that second and throw himself at her, declare everything that was in his heart and his soul. But what had he to give her and Harvest?

Nate could offer them so much more. She didn't want Richard. She'd made that plain. He shut his door, went upstairs and crashed straight onto the bed, hands balled by his side with frustration at Nate for pushing his way into their lives. There he lay, finally slipping into a fitful, black sleep.

★ ★ ★

Richard didn't believe in the power of dreams. He was much too sensible for that. Yet, as he awoke with the morning light shining through his window, he recalled the most vivid dream.

There was him, Flora by his side, her arm through his and baby Harvest lying in a sling over his shoulder. They were walking, stepping together in perfect harmony. He stopped, looked down and felt Flora's hand entwined in his. She looked at him with blue eyes full of love, and the little charm of the artist's palette with its multicoloured gems twinkled at her neck.

He planted a kiss on her forehead, and she nuzzled into him. He looked up and they were standing on a huge bridge looking out towards the impossibly tall buildings of a busy city, acres of glass windows reflecting the water of a harbour. That was it. Why hadn't he thought of it before?

This might be his only chance. At last he had an idea. He had to get to Flora before Nate Campbell did. Instantly, he sat up on the bed, seeing himself in the mirror opposite. His clothes might be rumpled with sleep, his hair tangled, but now he might, just might have a way to win Flora. It was now or never he thought, springing into action.

10

Flora jumped at the sound of her doorbell going. She hated confrontation but for Nate Campbell it was surely part of the cut and thrust of everyday life. She wished he wasn't coming. His visit yesterday had given her a sleepless night, but she had made her decision. Now she had to face up to it.

The doorbell rang again. She took one last look around the lounge. She had spent the morning tidying, clearing her mind by dusting every surface. The place looked and smelt spotless. The only thing lying around was the leaflet for the private school. Somehow it didn't have a place here and lay looking incongruous on the table.

Harvest was washed, powdered and dressed in a yellow all-in-one with a yellow knitted cardigan. As the doorbell rang more insistently, she was ready for him. She opened the door. Nate was the picture of confidence, feet apart, chin up.

'Glad to see you up so bright and early,' he swaggered in. 'A coffee'd be nice.'

'I've got the machine on already.' And the cups and tray laid out, everything ready, thought Flora.

Harvest was in her bouncy chair, sitting on the floor. As Flora brought the tray in, Nate was sitting in the armchair, leaning towards Harvest. In his hand he had an expensive looking pen, and something that looked like a business card. On the back he had written an 'H'.

'See?' he was saying, 'That's your initial, see, 'H' for Harvest.'

Flora raised an eyebrow. 'She's too young for that. She's only interested in playing.'

'They're never too young,' Nate stated. 'Scientific studies have proved that babies can respond to classical music in the womb. Like sponges, they

179

suck up knowledge.'

'She's just a baby.' Flora handed Nate a coffee and watched as Harvest took the business card in her sticky hand. 'Don't give her that, she'll only . . . ' But the inevitable happened and the business card disappeared into Harvest's mouth. Flora leapt over and took it out.

'That's the trouble with you, Nate.' Her voice was flat. 'You really don't know anything about babies, children — or people — do you?'

'Don't I? I know enough to make shedloads of money out of them.'

'But that's not everything surely.'

'Depends on who you are. Most people would say it's rather crucial.'

'Maybe, I'm not most people. You came here today to find out my decision on whether I want to go to New York under your wing so to speak, or maybe more accurately under your control.'

'I wouldn't put it like that.'

'Maybe you wouldn't — '

As Flora spoke, there was a ring at the door bell, far more insistent than Nate's ring earlier. This caller was jabbing at the doorbell.

'Excuse me.' Flora ran to see who it was.

'Richard! This really isn't a good time.'

'Flora, please let me in. I know Nate Campbell's here. That's why I'm here — I don't want you to talk to him without speaking to me first.'

'This is very difficult Richard. Can't we talk later?'

'No, Flora. What I want to say needs to be heard by him as well. Can I please come in?'

This new fired-up Richard was a revelation. There was something extraordinarily attractive about seeing a normally measured man electrified with emotion. Richard's eyes were flecked with gold fire.

Newly washed hair, thick and burnished, framed tanned skin and his eyes were hooded with intensity. This was a man with a mission. Dressed in a white t-shirt and jeans, his chest seemed wider than ever as he breathed deeply like a warrior going in to battle.

As Richard entered the lounge, Nate lifted one sardonic eyebrow. 'Oh, it's you.'

'Yes, I don't suppose you expected me to interfere with your scheming.'

'I don't know what you mean. What you think or do, Richard Cross, has very little bearing on me, Flora or Harvest as far as I can see.' Nate's eyes narrowed, his mouth an unyielding slash in a hard face.

Richard stood over Nate who remained seated. Flora got the impression that Nate wasn't quite as comfortable with the situation as he was trying to make out.

Richard said decisively, 'I'm here to prove you wrong.'

'Richard,' Flora tried to interpose, not wanting an ugly scene. She had made up her mind. Richard seemed to want to protect her but he didn't need to. She felt she was strong enough to live her life alone.

'Don't stop me, Flora. Because it's taken me a long time to pluck up the courage to say what I'm going to say. And if I don't make the most of this moment I may never be able to say what I mean ever again.'

'Then maybe it should be me who stops you.' Nate rose up out of his seat and squared up to Richard. 'Because Flora's coming with me. I made her an offer yesterday that no woman in her position would refuse. She's bringing Harvest and I'm going to pay for her to go to the finest school in — '

But Richard held up his hand and stopped Nate in mid flow. Richard's eye shot to the pamphlet and he snatched it up from the table, his face twisting as he looked at the words. 'That's what you're all about Nate Campbell isn't it? Money and privilege and buying your way into people's lives. Flora may have fallen for you, she may have been seduced by all that you can do for

Harvest but I can do a lot more.'

Nate smirked, a look of disrespect marking his sharp features. He shook his head. 'You? You're nothing. What could you do for her with your tiny house, your naff job and your boring domesticity?'

Richard breathed in. For a moment Flora's stomach knotted thinking he would hit Nate for insulting him. But instead, he turned and grasped her hands. 'Whatever he's offered you Flora, believe me it's nothing to what I want to give you. You're the best thing in my life. With you, everything's better. This last week has crystallised things for me. I always knew I loved you, from the second I saw you.

'I know what you told me about Damian, but I'm not like that, I want to give you so much. I don't want to take anything from you. Not your freedom, not anything that you don't want taken from you except your love.

'Damian was a taker and Nate is a taker. Believe me, whatever he's offered

184

you, it's all smoke and mirrors. It's the illusion of happiness. He wants to buy you and Harvest. He could never love you like I do. He doesn't want you like that, he just wants power over you and Harvest like he wants power over everything in his life. Don't let him in. Let me in. Choose me, Flora. Choose me.'

So saying, he took out of his pocket some sheets printed off the computer and handed them to her. 'I've booked these. I want you to follow your dream and I want to look after Harvest too. Let's go together. Tomorrow.'

Flora felt herself close to tears. A huge bubble of emotion welled up in her at Richard's words. With trembling hands she unfolded the sheets. E-mail airline tickets to New York, three of them, for her, Harvest and Richard.

She put her hand to her mouth and swallowed back the words. There were so many things she wanted to say, so many heartfelt thoughts but she couldn't find the words. Never before had she heard such an honest declaration. She knew Richard had found it hard to declare his love. He was taking such a risk. Suddenly, Nate's harsh voice invaded her consciousness.

'You're a darned fool Richard Cross, she's not going anywhere with you.' He picked up the leaflet and thrust it into Richard's face. 'This is what's really important — Harvest's future. And Flora's. I've offered to take her to New York myself to give her everything you can't. The chance to practice her art and meet the right people. I can give her commercial success on a scale she'd never achieve with you behind her, dragging her down.'

Now it was Flora's turn to speak.

This had to stop. She spun around to face Nate. 'It's just typical of you that you haven't even waited to hear my answer. You've assumed it's all sewn up, that the deal's in the bag. Well, let me tell you once and for all, you can't buy people. Not me anyway, and not Harvest.'

The baby looked up wide-eyed at the mention of her name, stunned into silence by the intensity of the adults' voices. 'My decision's made. I made it this morning while I waited for you, and when I read that leaflet again about that school. I suppose you thought I might not notice that it's a boarding school. I suppose you thought just because I hadn't met Harvest before last week that I couldn't have any real feelings for her, just like you don't have any real feelings for anyone. I suppose you thought I'd be delighted to palm her off to boarding school and nannies in the holidays.

'That's not the life I want for her. She caught my heart as soon as I met her, even though I didn't want her to. She's captivated and enthralled me and I've decided I'm going to keep her. What's more,' Flora turned to Richard, 'I can see you've fallen hook, line and sinker for her too Richard. If you're prepared to give up everything to take me and Harvest to New York, if you're prepared to start a new life looking after us both, if you really love me like you say you do, I don't care if we're hard up for cash because I couldn't care less how much money we've got. Because . . . because I love you too, Richard. I have for a long time, it's just that I felt I couldn't let myself because I feared you'd be just like Damian, or,' and here she looked pointedly at Nate, 'or just like him.

'Nate, you are one of the takers in life. You'd destroy Harvest. Please leave my house now.'

'You'll regret this. You're being stupid, letting your heart rule your head,' Nate growled as he picked up the leaflet and tore it to shreds. 'You've lost Harvest the best opportunity of her life.'

'No,' said Flora, 'Richard's the best opportunity she's got. A real father, that's what she needs, not someone like you who doesn't know the meaning of the word and thinks they can buy love.'

Nate slammed out of the house, and

the last they heard of him was his car screeching off down the road.

* ⭐ *

It was 6am on a jewel bright morning in July. An intense blue sky already held warmth, as Richard and Flora stood on the Brooklyn Bridge, watching a flaming orange sunrise break over the Hudson River. In Richard's knapsack was a picnic and their swimming things, all ready for the open air pool in Central Park. Harvest in her pram beside them waved her toy rabbit at the early morning joggers. The runners smiled at her, pounding along on the wooden boards of the bridge, their puffing audible as they thundered by. In a few hours, those same joggers would be in sharp city suits and sparkling white shirts working in one of New Yorks tower blocks.

Richard felt as he always did when he looked into Flora's eyes: that he would be happy to sink into their blueness for ever. He squeezed her hand. 'Don't the skyscrapers of Manhattan look glorious on these summer mornings? Just like some sleeping dragon slowly waking up.'

'They are superb.'

'They look even more superb in that fabulous painting you did. This city has really brought out the best of the artist in you. I'm so proud, not only that you sold your first set of paintings of the Manhattan skyline but for getting a commission too.'

'It's a dream come true. I couldn't have done it without you.'

'Me, I'm no artist. And I certainly don't think I'd count as an artist's muse. What have I done?'

She leant her head on his shoulder. 'You've made me happy. So, so happy. I've got you, and Harvest and New York. I never thought I could feel so complete. You know, I so desperately wanted to come here when I was lonely and single. But really, a bit of me was running away. Leaving home and running off to New York was a way of finding new meaning. I now realise I wouldn't have found that on my own. I needed you to make me complete, I just never realised it. How could I have been so blind?'

'Sometimes the things we really need are right there under our noses. You just have to jump in and take a risk.'

He bent down and placed a floppy pink sun hat from his pocket onto Harvest's golden locks to shield her eyes from the brightness.

'You weren't such a big risk after all Richard Cross,' Flora said as he straightened up, towering above her.

'And you two, Flora Cross and Harvest Cross,' Richard lifted Flora's hand to his lips and kissed the shiny gold wedding ring encircling her finger, 'You weren't a risk at all. You're what I always wanted. A family of my own.'

THE END

We do hope that you have enjoyed reading this large print book.

Did you know that all of our titles are available for purchase?

We publish a wide range of high quality large print books including:
**Romances, Mysteries, Classics
General Fiction
Non Fiction and Westerns**

Special interest titles available in large print are:
**The Little Oxford Dictionary
Music Book, Song Book
Hymn Book, Service Book**

Also available from us courtesy of Oxford University Press:
**Young Readers' Dictionary
(large print edition)
Young Readers' Thesaurus
(large print edition)**

For further information or a free brochure, please contact us at:
**Ulverscroft Large Print Books Ltd.,
The Green, Bradgate Road, Anstey,
Leicester, LE7 7FU, England.
Tel:** (00 44) **0116 236 4325
Fax:** (00 44) **0116 234 0205**

RACHEL'S COMING HOME

Gillian Villiers

When her parents run into difficulties running their boarding kennels, Rachel Collington decides to resign from her job and return home to help out. The first customer she encounters is arrogant Philip Milligan, who is nowhere near as friendly as his two collies. Gradually though, he begins to thaw — but just as Rachel is wondering if she has misjudged him, it seems that someone is intent on sabotaging the kennels' reputation.

HEALING LOVE

Cara Cooper

Dr James Frayne's personal life is in meltdown and it is beginning to affect his work. Becky, his Practice Manager, is deeply concerned and wants to help. But Dr James cannot afford to let her in on his secret — if she discovers what's troubling him, it could lose him his job. When his cold efficiency and her powers of deduction collide, sparks fly and emotions are stirred — changing both their lives forever . . .